T0156395

NIGHT STALKER I

– Trouble in New York City

By

PETER PERRY

Order this book online at www.trafford.com
or email orders@trafford.com

Most Trafford titles are also available at major online book retailers.

Printed in the United States of America.

ISBN: 978-1-4269-7215-7 (sc)
ISBN: 978-1-4269-7216-4 (hc)
ISBN: 978-1-4269-7217-1 (e)

Library of Congress Control Number: 2011909279

Trafford rev. 06/10/2011

 www.trafford.com

North America & international
toll-free: 1 888 232 4444 (USA & Canada)
phone: 250 383 6864 ♦ fax: 812 355 4082

Dedication

I would like to dedicate this book to my wife, Jessica, with heartfelt thanks, for letting me use our money to see the fulfillment of my dream in getting my book published.

You have no idea how much I love you, and would be nothing without you in my life.

TABLE OF CONTENTS

ACKNOWLEDGEMENTS

I dedicate this book to all of the people I love and care about the most in my life. You all know who you are. Through all of my years so far on this earth, never have I put the amount of effort into anything, as I have done in this novel.

I want to thank Clark Angelo, Kathleen Penafort and Gail Glenn, of Trafford Publishing; for sticking by me during thick and thin. Thanks guys for believing in me and my story.

I also want to thank Valerie Roosa, from Day Start Art Studios, for her editing services and great suggestions to make this story the best that it can be.

Last, but not least, I want to thank Melvin Harris, for the wonderful cover he designed for me.

And to anyone else I may have forgotten, thank you, and I hope you will all read my book over and over again.

INTRODUCTION

10:00 am June 16, 2005, Brooklyn.

The sweat pours off my face as I am racing my friend, Cody, down Main Street on my new bike that I just got for my birthday two months before. Mom and Dad have told me to not hang out with Cody anymore because he is a little rough around the edges, and his family are not like us…they are poor!

What an awful thing to say about someone, I say to myself, as I watch Cody fix his chain on his bike for like the fiftieth time on that beat-up old Schwinn, that was a hand-me-down from his brother, John.

John, of course, beat the crap out of the thing when he had it before he gave it to Cody. That bike has been to Hell and back, but Cody is persistent, and is determined to fix it and keep going.

He wants to beat me in the race...and he wants to get to my Grandpa Jim's, so he can have some of that delicious homemade lemonade.

"Come on Cody, Grandpa just bought me a new Play Station game, and I wanna try it out. Plus, he makes the best lemonade in the world! Put that chain back on and let's go!" I say to Cody as he keeps fumbling with it. His hands are now as black as tar and very greasy. I hope Grandpa don't mind us coming in a little dirty. He must have some kind of hand cleaner somewhere for Cody's hands after he's done messing around with his bike.

"Almost...got it...there! It should stay now...or at least until we get to your Grandpa's house.

How much farther is it anyway Jimmy? I think I'm sweating out the Kool-aid I had yesterday. It has been one hot day so far. How are you holding up Jimmy?" Cody says as he wipes the sweat from his forehead. The grease from the chain puts a nice black streak across his forehead and face. I laugh at him as he looks at me angrily and then pulls his Yankees baseball hat down over the top of the grease mark and gets back on his bike once again.

"It's about another half hour or so. It is not too much farther. I am doing all right, Cody. I know one thing, Grandpa better have a *full* pitcher of lemonade when we get there. Come on, let's pedal as fast as we can and see who gets there first!" I say as my mouth is getting drier by the minute, and my tee shirt is soaking wet with sweat. "I'm sure I don't smell too hot either."

The streets are packed with people, either going to work, shopping, or just on vacation, whatever. We both have to be careful crossing the road, traffic is out of control today. It is summer time and school is out, so it seems like everyone is out and about. Normal for this area, for this time of the year.

10:30am - Grandpa Jim's house

If it were any farther away, I probably would have had to bring a water bottle...and maybe a bagged lunch for Cody. He is a little bit bigger than I am...but he is a good friend just the same. My heart is racing, just as if I had ran the city marathon, as Cody stops quick right behind me...with his feet. I can hear the chain dangling around the bar again. I look at Cody and he just turns his hands over and gives me a, "oh well," look on his face.

As we stop in front of Grandpa's house it looks the same as it has since I can remember. The old brown wood type shingles, and the same mailbox that he must have had when dad was growing up. The lawn looks like it needs a good mowing and trimming, I thought. I'm sure his neighbors don't like the hay field that they have next door to them. Still...I love my Grandpa very much.

As we walk up the steps, a warm breeze blows but does nothing to cool us down. I knock on the door while holding the old-fashioned steel frame screen door open. It squeaks and makes a melody all it's own, as the wind blows through the screen and bangs the door into the side of my leg. I wait, and Cody stands beside me sweating, huffing and puffing from the race that he just lost. It wasn't his fault though, I blame it on mechanical malfunction, and not user error. We are both anxiously waiting for some ice-cold sweet lemonade, made with love.

"Hey Jimmy…Cody, whoa… it sure is hot out there today! Come in, come in, before you melt!

Have some lemonade before you get heat exhaustion or something," Grandpa Jim says, as he lets us into his house. On the kitchen table is an ice-cold pitcher of freshly made lemonade, with the humidity running down on the outside of the pitcher. Three cups are set on Grandpa's old oak table. Sure's not the same since Grandma Joan passed away three years ago. Sometimes it seems like three lifetimes, instead of three years. I don't remember her much, but Grandpa says she loved me very much.

Grandpa hasn't moved, or touched any of her things since she's passed. It is as if she is just on vacation, or visiting a friend. All of her knick-knacks are on the maple shelves Grandpa made for her some twenty years before. Her green flowered apron still hangs from the oven door handle as if she put it there yesterday.

"You boys have a good ride over? You both must be dying of thirst by now. Dig in, have a cup or two of my lemonade, I just made it twenty minutes before you got here. Also, if you're hungry, I have some chocolate chip cookies I made yesterday. I know they are your favorite Jimmy," Grandpa Jim says as I pick up a cup of lemonade, and drink it down in three big gulps. The cool refreshing liquid quenches my seemingly never-ending thirst. The air-conditioning feels good as Cody and I sit down and eat a couple of cookies. There is just something about chocolate chip cookies that I just love. Cody seems to be enjoying them too, as

Grandpa sits with us and begins to tell us some of his old stories of when he was young and would catch criminals for a living. He is still on the force, but he says he's going to retire in a year or two. His leg is hurting him more and more, and every time I come over to visit, he seems to be hobbling around and limping more on his right leg. Grandpa begins his story, as he pours another cup of lemonade and grabs a handful of cookies.

"So, there I was…forty years old…a homicide detective in New York City. At this time I had been with the 84th Precinct for oh, twenty years. I had solved many crimes and put away a lot of small time criminals, but this particular week had started with a murder of a young woman. Well… maybe I shouldn't go on with this story, it is quite gruesome. What would your mother say huh?" Grandpa Jim tells us, as he stops his story before it starts. He reaches for another cookie on his stoneware red plate…but it looks like Cody and I had a few too many, as the plate is empty now. All that is left on the plate are a few crumbs.

"Ah…come on Grandpa! Mom won't mind, because I won't tell her. I love hearing your old stories! You won't tell her will ya Cody?" I say, as I look at Cody. He shakes his head no, as he shoves the last of the cookies into his mouth. He slobbers all over himself and gets some crumbs and lemonade on his shirt. Grandpa and I laugh, as Grandpa grabs a towel and Cody cleans himself up. Grandpa thinks, and then continues his story.

"Well I guess it can be our little secret. I'll just cut out the graphic parts so you guys don't get grossed out, or scared. Anyways…where was I …oh, yes! So a woman was killed, but it wasn't that she was killed, it's *how* she was killed. No wound marks, no gunshots or anything. She was just...gone. As I dug deeper into the case, I later found out that she had died of a brain aneurysm. Not unusual...at least it didn't seem so."

"Who was she grandpa?" I ask him in the middle of his story. I like to get all the details.

"I'm sorry, Jimmy. That information is classified. I could lose my job if I tell you every detail of my stories. Okay, let's go on shall we?" Grandpa Jim says to me, as I sit back and focus my attention on his every word.

"I'm gonna fast forward a bit, so I can tell you the best part of my story, and then maybe I can fix you two some lunch. I came to find out that it wasn't a brain aneurysm, but it was caused by an unusual force. However, she wasn't the last victim to die of this strange occurrence. On top of all of the other crime that was increasing in the Big Apple, I had to deal with this one case that baffled me for the next few weeks, with three more victims falling to it. The last victim was the strangest of them all."

Grandpa Jim, continues telling us, as Cody and I are almost in a trance as we wait for the big finale, and the reason behind all of these helpless people. It's quite a bit of information to take in, but Cody and I are two kids who are ahead of their peers, and might even get to jump ahead a couple of grades. It would be so cool to be in second or third grade at seven years old. I don't mind Grandpas stories, In fact I find them fascinating.

"The last victim was marked with a black star on his face. He looked to be a businessman or someone very important to society, because he was dressed in a suit and had a briefcase in his hand. Inside the briefcase was documents that led us to do an investigation on the new company that was up and coming... Drakken Inc. Drakken Inc. led us to the owner, Thomas Drakken. I eventually put him in jail for murder and fraud, but he got out early because he was a vet in the Army, and he had been unwillingly experimented on early in his career. I think he just paid off the jury, but I will never know the real truth.

After his run in with the law, he lost his head and ended up going into hiding for a short time. Around the same time, strangely enough, a new enemy of the City's and mine, came onto the scene, his name...Black Star. He had all of these schemes to take over the world that kept blowing up in his face. I did eventually catch him again and put him back in jail where he belonged," Grandpa Jim says, as he looks at the clock on the kitchen wall.

"Oh well, it's getting to be lunchtime. I'm gonna make you guys some grilled cheese sandwiches. How's that sound?" Grandpa Jim says as he gets out a frying pan and some bread and cheese. He also cooks them in real butter. They just taste so much better in real butter, and not that fake oleo or that crappy spray butter that mom uses.

As Grandpa is in the kitchen making lunch, I walk down the hall and look around his house some more. He always has some cool things lying around, like books or statues or pictures. Past the hall and into the living room, I look at all of the pictures of Grandpa working on the police force. Some are of him when he was in his twenties, when he was still a rookie, all the way up to this year when he got an award for his forty years of serving the New York Police Department at the 84th Precinct. It's a beautiful picture of Grandpa Jim in the middle, with Commissioner Johnson on his left, and Mayor Harrison on his right, all of them shaking hands with the award on the table near them and big smiles on their faces. As cool as all of his pictures are, I have always been interested in getting into Grandpa's library room he's got in the back of the house. He keeps it locked up because he's got a lot of old books in there worth a lot of money. Some have been handed down from his grandfather and so on, and so forth, back a couple hundred years.

12:30pm - Lunchtime

There's nothing better than freshly made lemonade and grilled cheese sandwiches. Even after eating all those cookies, Cody and I are still hungry, and the sandwiches disappear rather quickly. Grandpa Jim smiles, and grabs the afternoon paper from the mailbox out front. Cody and I have one last glass of lemonade before we decide to take off back to Mom's house. We didn't get a chance to play that new game, but listening to Grandpa's old cop stories is so much better.

"Thanks for the lemonade and lunch Grandpa, but Cody's gotta get home. I do have one question though…whatever happened to that Black Star guy….is he still around?" I say as Grandpa rubs me on my head, and messes up my hair as we go back outside into the sweltering heat on this hot June afternoon.

"Well, Jimmy, he served his sentence in jail, and then somehow went back to his business. He is still there to this day, as far as I know. You boys have a good day now! Oh, Cody…you want some help with that loose chain of yours?" Grandpa Jim says as he steps out into the hot sun. He puts on his shades, and comes out to the bike. Cody and I help Grandpa fix Cody's chain on his bike, so that it doesn't fall off anymore. After about twenty minutes, we are ready to go. Grandpa waves us off, as we ride down Main Street and back to my Mom's house. What a day we had for sure! Cody gives me a high five, and walks his bike across the street and into his garage.

We stayed friends until the next year, when Cody had to move because his dad got a new job in Chicago. He was truly my best friend for the last three years.

To this day, I haven't seen him. I think he still lives in Chicago, with probably a wife and two kids, and a Beemer in the drive. It would definitely be a typical Cody with the BMW. He always liked luxury cars, and anything out of the ordinary.

12 years later - Grandpa's Funeral

I was in college when I got the call from Mom in the middle of the day. She said that Grandpa had been sick, but then he got better for a short while. Then, for some reason, he went the other way, and eventually he just passed on. I never felt such pain and heartbreak as I did when she told me he was gone. I took a week off, and went home to see how Mom was holding up. Even though it wasn't her father, she still had been close to him, and kept in contact with him, even after dad disappeared.

I had went out and bought a brand new suit with Mom, and did my best to prepare myself for the next day. I was to be one of the pallbearers, so I had to carry the casket into the church, and then back out again and into the hearse, after the service was over.

On the day of the funeral, it rained like it had never rained before. But I made it through, and even got up to say a few words about my Grandpa and how much he meant to me.

That was one of the most memorable times in my life…with Cody and my Grandpa. The weather we are experiencing now, reminds me of that time all of those years ago.

CHAPTER ONE

84th Precinct

1:00 a.m. New York City, October 2025

It has continuously rained now for the last twelve days. Large destructive drops hit heavy on the roof of the 84th precinct. As I look out the window, people are struggling to make it to higher ground.

A man trying to pull his daughter to safety is practically dragged down the street. The only thing that saves him is his umbrella handle, wrapped around a street light pole. His daughter, unfortunately, is among those who are swept away in the great tides of water rumbling through the streets. The man weeps and screams out in pain and grief, as everyone around him is trying to save themselves. The only thing the pedestrians can do, is watch and hope that it doesn't happen to them as they try to get to their destinations.

The water level has been rising two inches every day, and it is now so deep that mid-size sedans are floating down the streets. It's nothing to see BMW's, Chevy vans, and a few taxicabs rolling by among the havoc. The power has been out for the last eight days. People have raided the neighboring stores of any, and all, emergency candles and immediate supplies. Looting has been happening all over the city since the power outage first occurred. Street gangs have formed, and have been having a field day with all of the chaos that is going on. Dispatch has been so busy that they have not slept for three days. The way things look right now, it doesn't seem that they will get a break any time soon.

With just about every officer out on patrol, or doing rescue efforts with the Fire Department, I have been called in by Chief O'Reilly, to find some answers to this strange and unusual weather. Scientists and meteorologists from all over the State have been working on a solution to the cause of this tremendous amount of rain. They are the top in their field, and still they are all stumped and shaking their heads. So far, no one has come up with an answer. A group of scientists have even thrown around the idea that maybe Libya or Russia is behind this catastrophe, but after a few phone calls, those rumors are put to rest. I truly believe that there is *someone* purely evil behind all of this. Someone with a number of resources at their disposal, and the intelligence to make something like this happen on a grand scale. Two weeks ago, this new company has recently emerged called Drakken Enterprises.

The President of the company, Thomas Drakken, the third, some scientists from the State, and a few of Drakken's closest associates, were on television issuing reports of their testing of a weather machine. This machine would forever change the world, as we know it. It would bring back the light to this dark and dreary place. It was made to replenish our ever-shortening water supply, and to keep the human race going in the right direction. It had been locked up inside of the New York Science Building under the watchful eye of Roman Shangli, who is the head of Research and Development, and has been there for fifteen years. He understood what the project was for, and made it his life's work to guard its secrets. Somewhere along the way; money started running out.

The Federal Government has stopped funding Drakken's weather machine project due to lack of information and health issues. Suppose this machine got into the wrong hands? Then the world and all of its inhabitants would be doomed. Luckily for me, I am here to stop Drakken, or whoever is behind all of this, before it is too late. As of now... I don't have any leads, or information to put a case together against him.

I watched the telecast of Drakken's test, and he appeared to be a very impatient man, always wanting more no matter what the cost is. For some reason, my gut feeling is that he is the one who is our prime suspect. Of course, the Chief, Tom O'Reilly, would more than likely feel differently! He has yet to trust me on my hunches. He says, that I need to get more experience first, before I can judge others without probable cause. I do admire the old guy though...well...sometimes anyway. He has been on the New York

City Police Force for over thirty years now. He was made Chief after my grandfather stepped down due to his age, in 2005. You would think that O"Reilly would be ready to retire by now. In his early days, a couple of punk kids trying to steal a TV had shot him in the arm. They had fired several rounds, but all of them missed, except for that one. He also has been pushed down some stairs by burglars. He is a tough man though, and has the will and desire to not give up on anything very easily. He is tough on the outside, but an old softy on the inside.

This graveyard shift sometimes is for the birds, if you know what I mean. How can I have a life of my own when either I'm working, sleeping, or catching criminals that the NYPD could care less about? What has this world become when police officers pick and choose whom, and who, they are not going to arrest and put in jail? They must know more about this police business than I do, but I bust my ass, and they sit around and eat donuts all day! It's not fair…come to think of it…life ain't fair, but that's how it works sometimes. It's just my luck to get the shitty end of the stick.

Several times, I have seen criminals get a slap on the wrist because they know the judge, or paid off the jury. How fair is that! I guess it is not up to me to decide. Not me…the police officer anyway…if you know what I mean. There are things that happen in the night that no one knows about…or *wants* to know about… for that reason only. However, I keep a close tab on the judicial system here in my part of New York. If I see a criminal that needs a little extra kick in the ass, well, I just do it. I take the law into my own hands, when the law no longer works for the common good. Sometimes I get so carried away that I forget I am still a cop, but only during the day! It is a fine line that I tread on...it gets really difficult sometimes to know just where I belong.

The rain seems to fall with such force, and intent, that it almost seems...unnatural. Maybe there is more to this than even some weather machine...maybe not. I will do my best to find out all I can and stop this before it's too late. I am a Rookie cop however, so I have much to prove before I can move up the ladder. As I continue looking out the window at the heavy rains outside, I hear a familiar voice yelling at me from across the hall.

"Preston!" O' Reilly calls me into his office. Even the Chief himself has to be here in desperate times like this. He really is a strong man, even though he is getting up there in age. I think he is almost seventy...or maybe sixty...I don't know, and I don't dare to ask either! He puts a lot of faith in me for some unknown reason. I am nothing special, I do not think so anyway.

"You are new here, fresh out of the Academy just a couple of weeks ago," he says as he puts his feet on the desk. Chief O'Reilly can be so nonchalant at times, but still retains his professionalism.

"Yes sir, what can I do for you?" I say to him, as I make sure my belt is lined up and my shoes look clean and shiny. I am still quite nervous being how my grandfather served on the force. He once served as chief at this precinct from 1975 to 2005, just like O' Reilly is now. O'Reilly, of course, was just a Rookie back then.

He moved up the ranks… so I believe I can as well, as long as I keep my nose to the grind.

"Preston, I served with your grandfather and your father for a short time, and I just want you to know that I will personally help you and watch over you the best that I can. On the flip side of that, I want you to pay close attention to what I do, and follow through on the orders I give you. I expect *results* and you expect education…so we can help each other," O'Reilly says to me as he looks me straight in the eye. He is a very stern man sometimes.

"I want you to do a night patrol for me. We have had some complaints about noise and gang problems in a heavy populated part of Brooklyn. It would be a great opportunity to prove to me that you can be an upstanding officer like your grandfather once was. Be careful though, I have heard a new gang has formed in that area…I think they are called Scarab, but the details are minimal at this time. Take someone with you if you must… just don't get yourself killed huh!"

"Yes, sir, I've heard some of the same things myself."

"But it makes it difficult when the weather is still in a mess," O'Reilly replies, as I prepare to venture out into the pouring rain.

He sure does have a lot of faith in me… I wish I could say the same for myself. I grab my raincoat, rain boots, and my pistol from the storage area. I carry a 10mm but also a small caliber backup, just in case. I take my patrol car keys from the lock box, and walk to the front door. The rain is only a few feet from coming into the building. The drains are being overrun by the vast amount of water, so they are backing up, and most of the water has no real place to go. I'm surprised that the sewer system hasn't found its way to the surface yet, then we'll have a *real* problem on our hands.

CHAPTER TWO

1:42 a.m. outside of 84th Precinct

Science Building

Suddenly, just before I get outside, dispatch informs Chief O'Reilly that the Science Building is being robbed. So far, only a few details are known, only that there are four hoodlums in a futuristic car. They came right in through the front door without even smashing the glass or damaging the frame. That tells me that maybe they had a key, or it is an inside job. These hoodlums could be linked, or a part of this Scarab gang.

"Preston, that is in your district! Get on it, O'Reilly says to me as I head out the door and try to find a place to change into my costume. This is not a job for James Preston III; this is a job…for Night Stalker! I could probably handle the situation as a police officer, but then what would be the fun in that…I'd have to follow rules…and I *hate* rules! Night Stalker is a much better candidate for this type of situation. Plus I just *love* all the gadgets I have at my disposal.

I listen in to dispatch on the micro radio in my ear. Details now state that they got away with a Magnetic Energy Crystal Diffuser. This is a new device that some very renowned scientists were working on. It changes magnetic and static electricity into neurons of plasma energy. Why they would steal such a particular device is questionable, other than the fact that possibly the weather machine and Drakken Enterprises might be able to use it. Maybe it's the power source of the machine…the *doom* machine!

As I make my way to the roof to change into my 'outfit,' I can see two patrol cars head over to 15th street where the Science Building is located. The cold rain keeps falling as I put on my mask and activate my wrist communicator. It is my main line to my super motorcycle, Stalkicon. Stalkicon was a project that my grandfather and I had been working on for the past five years before he passed on in 2018. He had taken an old Kawasaki bike, and tore it down to bare bones, and then rebuilt it …well I did the work…he just told me where to put what…but it was a work in progress. Then time and his old injuries caught up to him and… the bike sat there for three years before I found his final schematics on it, and then finished it myself. It is the wave of the future… for crime fighting. With the most advanced weaponry and flight capabilities, it is my best work to date.

"Stalkicon, pinpoint my location and meet me here a.s.a.p." I say into my watch communicator. I once went to engineering college, with that, and the help from my father's old equipment; I redeveloped Stalkicon into the supreme crime-fighting machine it is today. Since I have owned it, I put on a Global Positioning system, and many onboard weapons.

"Affirmative, e.t.a. two minutes," Stalkicon responds back. I wait for my bike. I observe the officers below as they begin their investigation. I can tell that O'Reilly put most of us Rookies on the case, as a type of test. He just *loves* to mess with the new guys, and see if they can handle the pressures of crime in New York! Some make it...some don't. Most Rookies, he says, toss their cookies the first time they see a dead body...especially if it's all mangled up by some lunatic on a killing rampage. He loves to use metaphors to describe the ill fates of these young recruits.

Two minutes later, I arrive on the scene. The place is already flooded with police from nearby precincts. The lights flash and make it hard to see down the street. Just as I arrive, Special Forces and Chief O' Reilly show up. I knew he would want to see the rookie's handiwork with his own two eyes. He sometimes likes to get personally involved with the cases his officers take on, even though he's getting older, he's not out of the running yet. I step out from the shadows, and I surprise the Chief.

"Who the hell are you supposed to be? Some sorta superhero guy or something. Maybe *you* are the one behind this robbery. Lieutenant Jacobs, arrest this masked freak," O'Reilly says, as I back off and prepare to defend myself. I take a martial arts stance, and wait for them to make their move on me. I think about how they are outgunned because of my high level of training, so I decide to take a more diplomatic approach.

"Sir, I am here to help you solve this case. I am on *your* side. You have to trust me! I am Night Stalker," I say back to the chief, as I begin to walk into the Science Building. He looks at me with a stare that feels like his eyes are burning into the back of my skull. His gut feeling tells him that he should put me in handcuffs and then send me to the looney bin for evaluation, and maybe some drugs to bring me back to the *real* world. On the other hand, with the already chaotic environment that he, and everyone else is experiencing right now, maybe this masked hero guy is just what he needs to put all of this to rest, and get life back to normal. He'll just have to wait and let it play out.

"Fine...whatever! I will be watching you, but if you help us solve this cluster of a mess we got here, you will be okay in my book," O'Reilly says as he walks with me into the building. He pays more attention to me, and my outfit, than he does to his own people and where he is stepping.

"Let's get right to work then chief," I say as I roll up my right sleeve, and reveal my flashlight watch. Streaming light across the floor of the building, I could see where they had to drag the device for a few feet before they could load it into their car. The device looked like it was heavy because of the gouges in the cement, and the black marks from the bottom of their footwear, I estimate about 800 to 1,000 lbs. Then I see a piece of paper on the floor.

I pick it up and read it. "Dr. Shangli, 2020, New York Science Building."

According to a newscast I saw on this a few years back, Dr. Shangli and his associates developed this Diffuser to blast meteors out of the sky, just in case we were ever attacked. The City and State put up funding to compete with their neighbors. They all have similar devices at their command. Still the question that is on my mind is, what does this gigantic device have to do with the weather machine? Maybe there isn't any connection at all…and maybe there is. The clues just don't add up…not yet anyway!

Dr. Shangli and his associates have been missing for the last week now, just before all of this strange weather started, and right after the telecast with Drakken and his associates. Apparently, the police did not even get a call that they were missing. Shangli and his associates work on their own time. They come and go as they please…or whenever inspiration strikes them.

There was no time limit for this device, according to the State Government. They did keep the State up to date on details and progress, but no questions were asked. Shangli hated people bothering him with too many details and Government bologna. He figured that if he kept their mouths shut, then he could work at his own pace, and do what he wanted to do….even on a small scale.

"I think I may have found something, Night! Do you mind if I call you that, it's shorter and easier for me," O' Reilly says, as I walk over to him. "See that chip under the statue there? Do you think that could be of use to us?" He points at a small piece of plastic that seems to be stuck under the edge of this large metal and bronze statue.

"Yes, I believe so. Good job chief," I reply as I reach down and pick up a computer chip near the statue of Dr. Shangli. He is an important person in this building and in the State. His research and development team are known worldwide for all of their inventions and improvements they have made, here in New York City. Now, many years later, he is finally getting recognized for all of his hard work . It seems nice when one of the little guys gets his name in lights, instead of one of those Government ass kissers always getting their dues, and not even getting their hands dirty for it.

It seems that a chip has fallen out of the device while they were moving it out the door. If that is the case, then the device will not be functional, and they will be back for this. There is the possibility of this chip having nothing to do with the machine whatsoever, but my gut tells me different.

"I will hold onto this, if you don't mind. I also think I know who maybe behind this robbery, and all of the strange weather we are having," I say to the chief, as I put the chip in my secret pocket. I will have more luck finding out where it came from than the police. I have my ways of making people talk if need be. If I did give it to the chief, it would end up in some evidence room somewhere, and it would never be seen again. Not until it was needed, and then it would probably get lost…who knows with them! Not that I'm saying they are incompetent, but strange things sometimes happen when there are too many hands in the cookie jar. It's best if I hold onto it myself, and take it to the next level.

"Who do you think that is?" O' Reilly says, as he looks at me very oddly. He has no idea of my background, and who trained me to do detective work. I learned from the *best*, and I plan to be the b*est*. He directs some of the other detectives into some of the neighboring rooms as he waits for my answer. My grandfather taught me all he knows, he became my dad when my true dad disappeared all of those years ago. I try not to think of it, but it is hard not to sometimes, depending on what I am dealing with at the time.

"I believe it is Thomas Drakken, and/or Drakken Enterprises," I tell the chief, as the other detectives come out moments later empty-handed. They, of course, do not have the experience that I have. I have a knack for finding the smallest things, or the out of the ordinary things, in the strangest of places. I have always been able to do that since I was a small child, when mom would lose something and she would hunt for it for days, then I would find it before she did.

"Impossible! How can you say something like that? His company has made major improvements to our way of life. They helped fund the production of the weather machine to help keep pollution out of the air we breathe, and they made improvements to the water we drink. They helped in the research of modern day weaponry, and to nearly eliminate the need for traditional firearms. There is so much more that they will do ...and *can* do in the future. It's people like you who will put them out of business. You are way off! You better go back and do some real detective work...or you can leave it to us ...*real* police officers! We don't *need* to run around with masks and weird clothes on," he says, as he turns his attention from me, to his own detectives, who are still looking for clues or something to make them look important. They don't want to be a waste of taxpayers' money, but right now they haven't done a whole lot, just get in my way.

"Find anything boys, or are we just wasting our time here?" the Chief says to Tim and Seth, two detectives from the precinct, trained for crimes such as these. Tim, has about twelve years experience in homicide and robberies. He is a tall man with red hair and a bulging belly from too much beer. Seth, has about eight years of experience in robberies and forensics. He is shorter than Tim, and has black hair and a tattoo of a scorpion on his neck. He once served time in the State Prison, before he came to the Academy.

"I think we are done here, Night Stalker, go home and find another means of employment. Maybe you can join the circus or something. Drakken behind this? Pasha...no way in hell!" Chief O'Reilly says, as he laughs his head off and makes fun of me... *again*.

"Yeah, Tom, take a look at this," Tim says, as he hands to the Chief a small brass button. It's black, shiny, and about the size of a nickel. It has no markings on it, or company names. It looks expensive.

"Maybe we have something here," he says, as he brings it closer to his face. He almost puts it into his pocket but then I step in and give him my two cents worth. He is not pleased by it, but oh well…this is *my* job too!

"A button from a coat, or a pair of pants possibly," I say, as I look over the Chief's shoulder.

"Well, you know what guys, its 2:30 in the fricking morning, let's pack it up for now, and get some shuteye," the Chief says, as he puts the button in a plastic bag and then into his pants pocket. He then heads to the exit door. He looks at me again and shakes his head in utter disgust.

"Night Stalker, even thought I don't agree with you on your theory about Drakken, you still can help us and do some research on that computer chip. We will look into the button and see if there is anything to it, or what. If we need you again, how are we supposed to get in contact with you? I also am sorry about the circus wisecrack there, you know. I'm just not used to seeing masked hero type guys running around ya know. See ya, Night!" the Chief says to me, as he gets into his cruiser.

"I know how to contact you if I need to," I reply, as I head back to Stalkicon, and prepare to go home for the night. The Chief looks on, as I start to walk away and into the shadows. I am tired and need to rest. The morning will go by fast and it will seem like I will barely hit the pillow before it is time to get up again.

"Hey…Night, be careful out there…you may have potential yet," the Chief says, leaning out of the car window.

Luckily for the police force, they have air-jettison capabilities on their cruisers, so they are unaffected by all of the water. I wish I could say the same for the Science Building. The fire Department will have to deal with that later. The water is slowly seeping in and damaging everything in it's path. That is the least of my worries right now, as I have to begin doing some investigation into this chip, to see if it is tied in with Drakken Enterprises.

Suddenly as I make my way home, I see a dark shadow of a man in the distance. I think he has been watching the police and me, as we investigated the area. Why would he be watching us, and who is he? Friend …foe…neither! My heart rate increases and I keep on my guard.

I look in that direction again, and he throws something at me as I make my way into the night sky. I catch it, and it has some writing on it. I turn on my flashlight and look at the object. It looks like…a star. It is black and made of steel. Lucky for me it didn't cut into my hand or damage my bike.

"Hey…you…are you looking for me?" the dark figure says, as he now speaks from behind me. "I am the one you all are looking for, but…you will never catch me. I am the Black Star. I rule the night! I have for a very long time. I can't be stopped by these men claiming to be police officers…ha, haaaaaaaaaa….nor will I be caught by some 'wanna- be' superhero like you," Black Star says, as he makes his way into the night, laughing hysterically.

"Would you like me to pursue him, sir," Stalkicon says, as I watch him disappear.

"No, I am too tired. There will be a time and a place for that later on. Let's get home and get a few hours of rest. How in the world am I going to explain to the Chief tomorrow morning? I wasn't there at the scene last night. I'm sure he was counting on me."

"Stalkicon, take me home," I tell him as my eyes get heavy.

"Yes, sir, e.t.a. two minutes," Stalkicon says, as it fires its jets and propels us into the night once again. Evil will have to wait another day.

I head back to my townhouse that I use sometimes when I know that I will be busy for a while. It is located in the suburbs of New York. It is hidden from sight most of the time, due to the amount of trees that surround it. It has been in my family for years, going all the way back to my great-grandfather. I love the old place, it has such an eerie look to it from the outside. There's nothing that feels like home more than this place…well…maybe Mom's, but that hasn't been the same since Dad left.

With the new criminal who has risen to try to take control of the city, I have to study his moves, and do my best to figure out what his next move is going to be. On the other hand, the Chief will be looking for a good reason why I was not there last night.

I park Stalkicon in my underground garage that my grandfather and father built many years ago. The house and all of its contents were given to me when my grandfather passed away. I get into bed, and do my best to try to sleep, I will figure all of this out tomorrow.

CHAPTER THREE

Researching the chip - 9:00 a.m.

I call into work so I can concentrate on this robbery case as Night Stalker, not James Preston III. I hope the Chief understands that I am doing this for the greater good of New York City, and not for my own intentions. I get my belt and my outfit on, and head to some computer chip manufacturing plants in the area.

"Hello, I am looking for the machine that this would go into? If you cannot tell me that, then maybe the manufacturer," I tell the customer service attendant at the Hudson Chip Company. He looks at me funny, shakes his head, and then does his best work to answer my question as professionally as possible.

"Well…um…sir. It is definitely manufactured by us, but I do not know when, and I most certainly do not know what it goes into," he replies after a few minutes of research on his computer. "There's a Dr. Shangli at the Science Building who maybe able to help you more than I can."

"He can't, unfortunately…he was kidnapped a week ago… don't you watch TV or read the newspaper?" I say back to him, and head back to the city and go see the Chief.

I am sure he is in a great mood on this fine, Fall morning. His best new Rookie is home with a bad rash. Well, that is what he thinks anyway. I'll have to figure out a way to contract a rash before I go back to work. Sometimes my little white lies get the best of me, but I'll take care of it. I always seem to make my way out of a bad situation. I don't know if it is just luck, or my charm that convinces people to lighten up on me.

"Good morning, Chief," I say, as I make my way into the precinct. Everyone stops what they are doing, and watches my every move. Unsure of whom, or what, I am supposed to be. All they know is that I was there investigating the robbery last night. My strange outfit and weaponry keeps them occupied for a moment, and then they go back to doing what they were before.

"Good morning my ass, Night! Preston is home with some sort of rash he says, and we have five scientists still missing. Now, we have an even bigger problem besides the robbery. Take a look at today's news," the Chief says, as he hands me today's newspaper.

It reads "Two masked men flying in the air last night with unknown intentions. They maybe the blame for this foul weather, and the robberies occurring throughout New York. One is named, Black Star, and was last seen hanging around Drakken Enterprises early this morning, according to witnesses. His location is not known at this time. He is wanted for questioning. The other masked man is still at large."

"I will find out where he is, and put an end to this injustice," I tell the chief, as he and I head out, and I prepare to take to the sky on Stalkicon. "You know... the other masked man was me. I have nothing to do with all of what has been going on for the last few weeks. I was there with you last night."

"I know, but the general public doesn't know that. You have to try to keep a low profile until this Black Star is captured. You don't want to cause city wide panic do you? It wouldn't be good for you, or for me... the Mayor will be on my ass if you make headline news again!" the Chief says to me as I think about that button.

"I will do my best to stay out of the limelight, so we can keep all of the suits happy. Sometimes though, it is beyond my control. By the way, may I have that button? I wish to investigate that as well as the chip. Speaking of the chip for a moment, I found out it was made by Hudson Chip Company. The guy there couldn't tell me a whole lot about it though," I tell the Chief, and get on Stalkicon.

"Sure, but we want all evidence back when you are finished with it. I took the liberty of investigating the button's origin this morning. It belonged to a coat that was sold at Clarence's Coats, on 53rd street. It is about six blocks from here. Just be careful though, old Clarence doesn't take too kindly to weird guys asking strange questions around his place."

"Will do, Chief, I'll go check it out," I tell the Chief as I push the power button, and my jets start to fire up immediately.

"Be careful out there. Watch your back. That is a rough part of the city right there," the Chief says, as he is requested back inside due to an important phone call.

"Stalkicon, head to Clarence's Coats. I have entered it into your GPS system already," I tell him, as I check my weapons and adjust myself in the seat for quick takeoff.

"Affirmative, e.t.a. one minute," it says as it flies through the air and gets rave reviews from hundreds of spectators down below. They have never seen Stalkicon in the daylight before. His silver body gleams in the morning sun, as do his onboard weapons systems. He is equipped to the hilt with everything, from sidewinder type missiles and lasers, to front headlight mini guns. It is my favorite vehicle to drive, and I'm glad the general public enjoys my arrival on my bad-ass bike.

CHAPTER FOUR

Clarence's Coats - 10:00 a.m.

As I walk into Clarence's, I feel a sense of danger. Something is not quite right, like I am unwelcome in this establishment. The Chief was right,, this guy is suspicious of everyone. I hear someone come closer out of the corner of my eye.

"Hey, no freaks come into *my* shop and *live* to tell about it!" a voice from behind me says, as I feel a cold sharp blade shoved into my back. I swing around, and swiftly disarm him, as I look him straight in the eye. The knife clatters on the tile floor, as a surprised look suddenly comes over the man.

"Is that so, and who's going to tell me different?" I say to the man, as I grab my stun pistols from their holsters and stick them in his face. He begins to back off and raises his hands into the air above his head. He slowly bends down to pick the knife back up, the whole time we are keeping eye contact with each other. He knows that I am able to beat him any day of the week.

"I am Clarence Simmons," he says. I stand there and he moves back behind his counter and puts the knife away. I guess he feels safe with that blade-- old fool!

Suddenly he pulls out a short sword-- comes out from behind the counter, and lunges towards me. I maneuver him out of the way, quickly disarming him as he falls to the floor with a thud.

"Now you were saying?" I ask him, as he picks himself up off the floor and puts the sword back under the counter. He's not quite sure who I am, or why I am there.

"hmm…what do you want with me, freak?" Clarence says, as I push him up against the wall. My arms swell inside of my suit as he gets a scared look in his eyes. His breathing becomes erratic, and his eyes shift back and forth like a scared animal looking for a way out of its cage.

"I'm looking for the owner of a coat with black brass buttons on it, like this one here," I tell him, as I show him the button that was recovered from last night. Good thing I brought it here, instead of the Chief.

" Hmm…if you let me go, I'll check my computer and be able to tell you what you want to know…just don't hurt me," Clarence says, with a slight hesitation in his voice.

If I wanted to hurt him, I could have done so when I first walked in. He sure did change his tune real quick after I roughed him up a bit.

24

"Okay, but no funny business…or else!" I tell him, as he goes back behind the counter and starts typing away on his computer. He is shaky as hell, but he is diligent and precise.

Five minutes later, I am still waiting for an answer from Clarence. I wonder if this is a dead-end or not? If he were worried about me hurting him, he would have notified the police by now.

"Here we go; Herbert Mumfield, was the last person to buy a coat like this from me," he says to me as he continues to type on his keyboard. He seems like an upstanding citizen. If there was only more like him in this world. I guess he was just trying to protect himself and his business from 'so-called' freaks…like anyone would.

"Very good, how long ago was it?" I ask him, as I keep a close eye out for his customers.

"About three weeks ago he came in, a middle-aged man with graying hair. He paid with cash, that's about all I know," he says back to me.

Finally, a good lead I say to myself!

"Okay, thanks! Now…next time I come in here, you're not going to give me *any* trouble …right?" I tell him, as I look him sternly in the eye.

"You got, it Mister," he says, as he runs into the back of his store. He looks at me one last time from behind the curtain, before I leave out the door and head back to the station.

11:45am - the station

"Hey, Chief, I found some out some more information on that button," I say casually as I walk into O'Reilly's office. He is on the phone with the Mayor. He is trying to explain what happened last night at the Science Building.

"Yeah, what's that? Make it quick. The mayor does not like waiting," O'Reilly says, as he holds the phone away from his ear, as the Mayor chews his head off. The Mayor is quite upset by my high flying antics last night, but how was I to know I would make front page news. His main concern should be Black Star, and *his* intentions. Of course, I'm not a politician, so I guess bad guys on flying machines are of no concern, just what he looks like in the public eye, and to make sure that when voting time comes around he is the winner...and no one else.

"The button belongs to a Herbert Mumfield," I tell the Chief. He is still trying to recover from the Mayor who ripped his ass in two...verbally.

"Mumfield...why does that sound familiar?" the Chief says, as he punches the name in the police database. The police database has every known taxpayer; criminal; businessman, in the city. It is the most advanced and widely used system in the precinct.

"Here it is...Herbert Mumfield. He works at the Science Building with Dr. Shangli. Well, he did anyway. He must be one of Shangli's assistants that got kidnapped with the rest of them," the Chief says, as he looks angry because of the kidnappings. He wishes he could do more, but he doesn't want to push himself too much. That's why he has younger people doing most of the footwork for him.

"Now it's all coming together..." I say, as the alarm goes off throughout the station. This is a major incident apparently. That is the only time the alarm sounds. If there is a radiation leak or a bomb threat, that's the main reasons why it would sound off.

"Trouble at the nuclear power plant...six goons and one guy dressed in black attempting to steal a chip...they appear to be armed and dangerous...request full support," Dispatch says.

"Black Star," I say under my breath, as I check my weapons and prepare to head to the nuclear power plant. I watch my fellow officers grab their stun rifles and head to their cruisers.

"You coming, Night? We could use every able bodied person on this. This is major!" the Chief says to me, as he cocks his rifle and heads towards the door.

"You better believe it! I am on my way!" I tell the Chief, as I head out the door to Stalkicon.

"Emergency...set locators to nuclear power plant...let's go!" I tell Stalkicon, as I fire up the rockets and ascend into the sky.

"Affirmative...setting locators to the nuclear power plant... all weapons operational and ready...e.t.a....one minute, thirty seconds....checking and sending info to any air traffic to re-route if possible," Stalkicon says, as I duck my head down and give full power to the rockets.

"Dispatch...this is Night...any more info on the situation at the power plant?" I say into my wrist communicator. Any more information will help me to prepare for a battle with Black Star and his goons.

"Sorry…that is all we have, Night, wish I had more," dispatch replies back.

"That's okay…I'll manage, I'm sure. I just hope I can do what I am supposed to do, and no one gets hurt in the process," I say back to dispatch, as I continue flying towards the nuclear power plant.

"I'm sure you'll do fine…good luck, Night!"

CHAPTER FIVE

Nuclear Power Plant - 12:30 pm

As I get closer to the plant, I can see Black Star flying around the smoke stacks…waiting.

Waiting for what I do not know. I don my cape, and stop in front of the power plant. The water table is not as high here, because it sits up on a hill on the outskirts of New York. I usually don't wear my cape as it tends to get in my way, but for some reason, this time it just seemed right…and it looks fricking cool with it's shear black shade, and ability to take a bullet and reflect it back to its enemy. I think that is so damn cool!

"Stop right there, Black Star…the chip stays here," I say, as I pull out my stun pistol and prepare for battle. I can see now that it was me he has been waiting for…lucky me, huh…got some lunatic for my fan base. I take a martial arts stance and keep my pistol on him.

"So …you came! I thought you would just whimper in shame after I got away with the computer chip from the Science Building…oh…did I say that out loud? I didn't even think you would even show up…this is *wonderful*," Black Star says, as he descends to the ground.

"Now how are *you* going to stop *me* from taking the chip, and becoming the most *powerful* man on earth?" he says, as he lands and prepares for a fight.

"I will stop you anyway I can." I say to him, as he lunges towards me. His fist connects with my face as I try to dodge out of the way. The pain is almost too much to bear, as I drop my pistols. They land on the ground with a *clunk* about ten feet from me. Totally out of my reach from where I am at the moment.

I attempt to retaliate with my own move. A kick to the head drops Black Star on the ground. I quickly move and pick up my pistols and point them at him, as he laughs hysterically.

"Had enough yet? You stay right there until the proper authorities show up," I say to him, as my fingers are on the triggers. He just smiles at me with that cocky look, like he has already won. The only thing I'd like to see him win is an extended stay at the maximum prison for, oh, thirty years or so.

"*Never*! I have only just begun, Night Stalker, you are a fool! While I am out here playing games with you, my associates are inside doing all of my dirty work…for me," he says to me.

He takes another swing at me. As he misses me this time, I punch him in the stomach and as he doubles over, I give him an elbow to the back of the head. He drops to the ground once more, and grabs his electro club from his belt. He then touches me with it and takes me off my feet. He holds me to the ground and attempts to choke me with it.

"Look at you. You are no match for me! Give up yet...you sorry excuse for a superhero...more like super zero instead," he laughs at his own insults, as he is choking me.

"*Never*...You will *never* win!" I say with a gargle in my voice. My throat hurts as I grab his club, flip him off me, and throw the club away from him. It lands in a small grove of trees near the edge of the high cliff that drops to the ocean below.

Another kick in the head, and I grab my stun pistol and fire it at him. It sizzles on his black suit and he drops to the ground one more time. He stays still for a few moments before he starts to move around again and tries to get back onto his feet.

"I can do this all day," I tell him, as I watch him slowly start to get up. He is breathing heavy now, like he is exhausted. Guess he's not in as good a shape as he thought he was.

Black Star gets up, shakes what's left of my stun blast off, and flies into the air. He takes a downward spiral swoop like an eagle, and fires an electro-line from his wrist launcher. I try to out-maneuver it, but it captures me before I have time to react. I had no idea he could fly on his own power.

When he lands I can see it takes a lot out of him, and he has to stop and catch his breath. I look at him, and his eyes are all weird and bloodshot. His face is pale and it looks like when he uses his powers, it drains his life out of him or something. This could come in handy down the line. After a few minutes, he has regained his strength...and his loud obnoxious mouth.

"Ah hah, now who has who?" he says, as I fall to the ground. I am powerless as I watch for the Chief and the other officers. For some reason, it is taking quite a while for them to arrive. The power of the line is draining the energy from all of my weapons. I try to alert Stalkicon, but my wrist communicator does not respond.

As I try to reach into my pocket to get my cutter, I wonder if he is more of a match for me than I realized.

"Got it," I say as I cut my way out of the line. I grab my pistols from the ground and fire two more powerful blasts at Black Star. He moves out of the way, but the blast from the second pistol hits him full in the chest. He falls to the ground; and this time does not move. The blast I'm sure didn't kill him, but it will immobilize him ...hopefully long enough for the cavalry to arrive.

"It seems that good always triumphs over evil," I say, as I begin to round up his goons. Some of them had come out of the building, but they were too late to try and do a sneak attack on me.

As I start to head into the building and look for some more play toys belonging to Black Star, I hear the sirens in the air from the cruisers. The Chief and his men flood the scene. It's good to finally see some of them actually doing their job! Just in time too, as I was starting to wonder if I was all alone in this venture.

"Good work, Night, I may have underestimated you," O'Reilly says, as he puts cuffs on Black Star and pushes him into the Swat van.

"Thank you, O'Reilly, but it's not over yet. His goons are still inside," I say back to the Chief. "Oh, there's one more thing I need to do. I'm sure that you and your men have it under control from here," I say to O'Reilly, as my mind now goes from here to the fate of Shangli and his associates.

"Go ahead, Night, we got it...and thanks for your help!" he says, as I make my way back to Stalkicon.

O'Reilly and his detectives, head into the building and round up the goons inside. Down the hall, they catch two of the goons trying to steal a nuclear power rod. They grab their guns and fire in the direction of O'Reilly and Seth. Seth moves out of the way, but O' Reilly is hit in the shoulder.

Ted and Tim, chase after the other four goons as they are trying to steal the chip that Black Star needed so badly. Automatic gunfire, and two quick blasts from the officers' stun rifles, makes quick work of these wanna-be bad guys.

"Got them in the van! Chief. how you doing?" Tim asks, as he gets into the cruiser.

"Okay, just wondering where Night had to go?" he says back to Tim.

"I'm not sure Chief, but I bet it's important!" Tim says, as they both look up into the sky and back towards the city.

CHAPTER SIX

Drakken Enterprises

Off to the penthouse suite of Drakken Enterprises I go, trying to prove my theory. There I find Dr. Shangli and the other associates tied up and gagged. I also find the weather machine.

"It's Drakken, he has gone mad. He has built himself this super suit and calls himself Black Star," Dr. Shangli says, as he looks at me in awe. I cut his straps from his hands. He rubs his wrists and tries to ease the pain from the marks that they caused.

"How do we shut this stupid machine off?" I ask the good doctor, as he starts to untie his feet.

"We simply have to find out what powers it and dismantle it," Shangli says, as he unties the rest of his associates. They are scared, and run to the first exit door they find. They take the elevator to the bottom floor. They hop into the first emergency vehicle they find, and head to the precinct.

"We have to find the power source before 3 p.m., which is when it will unleash most of its power on the city, then it will self destruct! That's how Drakken wanted us to build it," Shangli says back to me.

"It's 2:55, we have less than five minutes to find the power source and shut it down," I say.

I look at the machine. A large beam of light flows from the front of it into the sky. It apparently manipulates the clouds, and increases the amount of rain that falls to the ground. There are multiple switches on it for different kinds of weather.

Suddenly, I see a small red button near the front of the machine. It is locked inside a small transparent box. Without a key to open it, all could be lost. All of New York City could fall into the ocean.

"Could this be the power switch?" I say as the doctor looks at me.

"Yes, that's it! Hit it, and the machine should begin its shutdown process," Dr. Shangli says, as he finds a place for cover... just in case something happens! He finds an old drainpipe, and hides behind it.

As I press the button, the machine makes this slow, winding noise, and the beam emitting from the machine becomes smaller and smaller in diameter. The power has been shut down... hopefully ...for good.

"There, I think you have done it, Night!" the doctor says with excitement and relief in his voice. The machine has finally stopped, and New York City and the entire world will be safe once more.

CHAPTER SEVEN

84ᵀᴴ Precinct again

4:00 pm

Back at the station, O'Reilly and his men celebrate another victory in the fight against organized crime. In the power plant, they also found the M.E.C. device. This magnetic electro control device could have been used by Black Star to advance the settings of the Doom machine, as Black Star called it. It would have created worldwide chaos, and odd weather all over the earth for decades to come. Even to the extent of the end of the human race. Fortunately for us we found it in time, and successfully turned it off.

The device will be returned to the Science Building with 'level five' securities intact. Dr. Shangli, and his associates, can study it more and use the machine for the common good of man. It will never come in contact with Black Star, or any of his cronies again.

I, on the other hand, decide to dismantle the Doom machine further, and spread its components all over the world. If it is separated in pieces, it will make it more difficult to find and to put back together again.

Meanwhile, City officials and volunteers begin to drain the city, and start opening all of the floodgates. They set up these large pumps and hoses and pump the water back into the ocean. It may very well take a month or two, but soon our beloved city will be back to normal once again.

Back at the prison, Black Star awaits his trial. He still thinks he has won, but little does he know that Night Stalker will always be there…to stop him from all of his evil plans to rule the world.

"I'll get you, Night Stalker! You have not heard the last from *me*! I *will* rule the world! Ha, ha! Ha, ha! Ha, ha!" he screeches out wildly and insanely, as he is brought deeper into the prison, awaiting his sentence. The prison guards take him to the maximum-security section. Here he will be surrounded by guards and video surveillance twenty four hours a day. A special pass key is needed to enter the area where he is being held.

His sentence is twenty five years without parole! As much as he hates being in prison, he hates more the fact that he was defeated by Night Stalker, and vows to make him pay for the embarrassment, no matter what the cost.

CHAPTER EIGHT

The Predator Jet

I arrive at the precinct the next day. Everyone stares at me, as if I am some sort of disease. I am prepared to take the heat from O' Reilly when he sees me this morning.

"Preston, my office *now*!" O' Reilly says to me, as I try to sneak past his office without him knowing. He is really upset with me. If he only knew, I was there that night, not just as Preston.

"Ye...ye...yes, sir," I stammer, "Preston reporting for duty," I say, as I salute him. I try to hide the bruise on my face but...too late!

"Hey Preston, where did you get that bruise? Your girlfriend beat you up or something," he says, as he looks at me with guns in his eyes. "You blew it the other night! Where the hell did you run off to? You said you were on your way there, then...nothing...

no show…no call…*nothing*! I depend on you, like I do all of my rookies, but if you can't do the job, then maybe you need to find other employment! Your grandfather and father, are probably turning in their graves knowing that you have disgraced your family's good name in this precinct! Well, what do you have to say for yourself…huh…speak up boy," he says to me.

"Well…sir…there was another robbery that was just as important to look into, then I lost track of time…and well… hmm…I have no excuse for not being there…I'm sorry," I tell O'Reilly, as I put my head down and hope that he can forgive me.

"I will let it go this time. Only because…and hear me out… your family put a lot of blood, sweat, and tears into building up this precinct to what it is today.. Your father…well…let's not get into that right now. I'll let you off you this time, just make sure that when I give an order next time, you carry it out to the tee… do you understand, Rookie?" he says as he leans back in his chair, and puts his feet up on the desk.

"Yes, sir, I understand completely, but I was…" I start to say to him, and try to weasel my way out of trouble. Rumor has it that, if you make O'Reilly too mad, he will put you on meter-maid duty, until you feel like wearing a dress yourself.

"You were disobeying an order is what you were doing, don't let it happen again! Take the rest of the day off and think about what you did, and come back to work tomorrow ready to do some police work…under *my* rule," he tells me, as he gets out of his chair and looks at some old pictures of my grandfather and himself from years earlier. There is one with both of them, with Mayor Harrison and Commissioner Johnson, in it . It is from a dinner party during Grandpa's last year on the force as chief. O'Reilly looks at it, and then at me, with that look of disgust, and then with sympathy. Not something you see everyday from the Chief.

"You know, Preston, your grandfather was a good man...the *best*! He would charge into a building outgunned, outnumbered, outmatched in every way, and still come out on top. No one will be able to do what that man once did...and I miss him! He not only was my boss...but a friend," O'Reilly said, as he looked away from me and down to the street below. I think he may be crying, or going to cry, but he is too old-fashioned and proud to let me see him in that vulnerable state.

"Do the best you can Preston, and you'll go far! Now, go... enjoy your day...and be back tomorrow...ready to work," he says to me, as he makes his way back to his desk .

"Sure, Chief...I'll see ya tomorrow!"

I make my way out of his office. Everyone still staring at me, as I walk past them all and head home to think. As I am actually heading home, I can do some more tests on my new weapon. It is called the Predator 5000 super jet. It is a two-person mini-jet with full armament. It has shields that can protect it from regular gunfire and energy fire. I hope that in the next few weeks it will be ready to test on some *real* criminals.

I get home and find that the daily newspaper, as well as all of the news channels, are filled with the happenings at the power plant and the Science Building from last night. Some of what is on there is true, and some of it has been fabricated by this new broadcasting station called, The Real Truth. It is apparently operated by...are you ready for this....Kelley Drakken. She is the wife of Thomas Drakken II, the previous CEO of Drakken Enterprises. As everything that he created now falls by the wayside, because he went crazy and became Black Star, she is trying to keep the family's glory going by creating real news, but with her input added as well. Of course, just a bunch of lies and hidden hatred for what the NYPD did to her husband. It apparently is making some real presence in the ratings, and is heading for the top five spot. Crazy how a show full of crap could actually be more popular than a *real* show like, Crime Syndicate...a real life cop show with actual story lines. I don't think that The Real Truth will last...but hey what do I know?

I go down to the basement of my townhouse, turn off that awful news station, and do some testing on the Predator. It is green and black, with a darkened front windshield on it. It has shortened wings which can fold up, much like a harrier jet from days of old.

The weapons systems are top of the line. I invested much of my family's money into companies that made me a millionaire ten times over, much to my chagrin. I still enjoy working a regular job though, just to keep people from landing on my doorstep and begging me for money. Only my closest friends know the truth about me…and I hopefully can keep it that way.

The Predator carries four on board ATL missiles, and two ATS missiles, that can do substantial damage. It has six forward firing gun tubes . Two are stun, two are laser, and two are 30mm chain guns used many years ago. I still like some of the old technology from my grandfather's days. It seems to be much more reliable in the field, but then it depends on the situation. It makes more noise and pumps you up more, when you hear gunfire versus laser beams. It's just not the same. Something about the smell of gunpowder that is manly, and boosts your testosterone levels beyond what they are supposed to be. It is an *awesome* feeling to have that kind of power in my hands.

Dr. Shangli actually has been helping me since I saved his life from the hands of the insane criminal, Black Star. He is actually very intelligent and helpful, if you keep him off the Scotch Whiskey. He likes to drink it straight. He tells me that it helps him think more. I think he just likes the taste of it, and it helps with his nervous twitch in his neck. It drives you crazy if you watch him for any period of time. Still, his mind works just fine.

If we keep working on it, and running more flight tests and weapon simulations, it should be ready by next week. I have been patient for the last few years, waiting to have a companion for my first weapon /vehicle, Stalkicon. It will make a wonderful addition to my arsenal I think.

CHAPTER NINE

New York Maximum Security Prison

November 2025

I figure I would go and see Thomas Drakken, aka, Black Star, and see how he is holding up behind bars. I don my suit, and get Stalkicon ready for takeoff. Dr. Shangli knows of my secret, so I trust him with all that I have to guard the house while I am gone. He is a scientist at the Science Building by day, and works for me by night .

"Hello there, Jim, how's it going ?" I ask the gate guard. Since I have been on TV, I now have a following of. ..you may say…fans, who admire my bravery and courage for what I did for the City.

Some would not agree, and think I am here to destroy the City, but many others believe that what I do is just, and right. Jim is one of those followers. Gotta admire a man who can speak his mind, and still work for a department of the Government. It takes balls to do something like that.

"All right, I guess, Night. What can I do for you today?" he says back, as he looks at my stun pistols. I bet a part of him would love to take a few blast offs with my stun pistols, and go on a shooting spree like a cowboy out in the old west. Then again, I could be wrong, and maybe he is just wondering what I plan on doing with them.

"I'm here to see Thomas Drakken the third, or Black Star, whichever you prefer?" I say to him, as I prepare for what I am about to do.

"Of course, Night, but you must remove all of your weapons, and leave them with the guard once you step through this door and the x-ray machine," Jim says, as he uses his thumbprint to open the door for me. He plays with his baton, and dreams of being a vigilante like me someday. I wonder if he has a picture of me up in his house somewhere? Nah…that would be too weird… even for him!

"Thanks Jim, will do," I say reluctantly," you have a nice day," I say as I enter the prison, and leave everything with Rick and Travis, at the next entryway. "You guys don't play with that stuff now, you have no idea what they are capable of. They can take your hand off, or stun you until ..well…just don't touch them!," I tell them, as they open up the next door for me into the prison.

"Sure, Night stalker, we won't touch any of it, you can trust us on that. Mr. Drakken is the last cell on the right. You can see and speak to him through a small window in the door," Travis says to me.

"Thanks, Travis, you had better heed my words," I say jokingly, as I walk down the long hallway.

In the back of my mind, I have this funny feeling, but maybe it's because I am about to talk to a mastermind criminal, who has been here for a month now. Without his little pions to do his dirty work for him, he must be totally lost. He is a businessman after all, and probably has had a lot of experience with delegating his orders and instructions. A pencil pushing job for the most part.

This prison makes me feel very uneasy. The sounds of men discussing Drakken's plots of revenge fill the air. What could a man of once great stature have happen to him that would make him hate the world so... and now...me too? Is it from a bad childhood? Maybe his family and mine know each other from way back when, or something ? These are all questions that run through my mind as I make my way further into the prison, and in to see that maniac.

Suddenly, an alarm sounds off, as I rush to Black Star's cell. His door is surrounded by five guards, shaking their heads in amazement. They can't believe what they are seeing with their own two eyes.

" What's going on here?" I ask, as I look in and see Drakken's body lying on the floor. A small trickle of blood is flowing from his mouth. His eyes are glazed over and glossy. I have one of the guards open up the door for me. Even though he is probably dead, I have to take all precautions and keep on my toes, just in case it's a trick for him to try an escape from the prison.

"Looks like suicide to me," one of the guards say, as I search the cell for clues.

There is nothing in here he could have killed himself with that I can see. Two of the guards are inside the cell with me, either out of curiosity, or to protect my ass…not sure which.

" Could be, but then again, he could've had a hit out on him," I say back to the guard. As I look closer at the body, I see a small hole in his neck. It is from a small dart that pierced his jugular vein, but all of the blood stayed inside the body. The blood on his mouth comes from the head wound he got as he hit the floor.

"Ah, what do we have here?" As I look down, I see something near his left hand, a small piece of paper with a series of numbers on it. 515-109-672 is written on it. "Could be a combination to a safe, or an activation code of some kind," I say to the guards as I walk back out of the cell.

"I can tell you what happened here, but I'll leave that up to you guys to figure it out instead," I say, as I walk down the corridor with the slip of paper in my hand.

"Wait…wait…Night," the guards protest. "Just tell us now… otherwise we will be scratching our heads and doing paperwork on this scumbag till next year," Travis yells to me as I am almost out of that section of the prison.

"Well, Travis ol' boy ..I will tell ya! Black Star…Drakken… whatever you want to call him, had friends on the inside, or so he thought. He thought he could trust them, so he told them of his plan of escaping and trying to reassemble the Doom machine. When they wanted money, well…you can guess the rest…so they bumped him off.," I tell him as his eyes get big, and he listens to every syllable that comes out of my mouth.

"How…what…who? How did you know all of that?" Travis says back to me in amazement. He is so Neanderthal, it makes me sick to think that our gene pool has not advanced beyond this type of human being. He should have picked a different career instead, like sanitation, engineer or something. Not saying that I have a thing against garbage men, but let's face it, they aren't the smartest dudes on the planet…you ain't gotta have a college degree to dump the world's trash! Come on!

" Well, I have been doing this a lot longer than you have sonny boy, so let us just say that good detective and police work runs in the family," I say to Travis, as I get to the desk and put all of my gear back on.

The guards look at all of my stuff as it goes back onto my suit… back where it belongs…in capable hands.

CHAPTER TEN

The townhouse / further
investigation - midmorning

I head back to the townhouse, and start to look further into the dart that I pulled out of Drakken's neck. I took the liberty of taking a sample of his blood to the lab here in the city. By tomorrow, I should have the results back. The dart was actually a small tube of hard plastic that was fabricated here in the prison, and used as a weapon. By whom, I have yet to find out?

"Find anything yet, Night?" Shangli asks, as he puts the finishing touches on the Predator jet. "This should be ready by Monday to take out if you need to, Night," he says, as he is leaning into the cockpit and checking on some of the electrical components one last time.

He is a great man in my mind. Without him, none of this would have been possible in the amount of time that it was accomplished. I just wish that the City would commend him for all of his hard work he has done. Maybe someday, when the shit hits the fan again, they will see him and his true talents for what they are.

"I found a small dart lodged in the neck of Drakken. I also found a small piece of paper next to him with these numbers on it." I pull out the paper and show him both of the items. He stares at them for a moment, turning the dart over and looking inside of it, smelling it even…what a weirdo…but he knows his stuff though.

"The dart looks like it has some sort of liquid in it still, like it has some sort of poisoning properties to it. The numbers could be anything. What is so strange is that he died while in prison surrounded by all of those guards and surveillance. How did this all come about?" he says to me, looking puzzled by the whole situation. Shangli is quite intelligent, but even he sometimes can be stumped by the odd occurrences in this world.

"I think it is an inside job! One of those guards at the prison, seemed rather peculiar and shaky to me. His name was, Rick. He just wasn't acting right. Let us see what kind of dirt we can dig up on this guard? Maybe, he is not a guard at all," I tell Shangli, as he keeps staring at the numbers on the paper.

"Night, maybe the numbers add to something, or mean something in that sense?" he says back to me, as I further analyze the dart.

"Hey, I may have found something here. There *is* poison on it. It derives from rat poison. How is it possible that rat poison got into the prison facility?" I ask him, as he sips on his freshly brewed coffee, lots of sugar, very little cream.

"So what you're saying is that if you add up all of the numbers on the paper, then they spell out a name or a word?" I say to him, as I sip on my Captain and Coke. It is my favorite drink. It helps me to ease my mind from the everyday stress I have to deal with.

I start to play with the numbers more and more, but come up empty-handed. As the day turns to night, Dr. Shangli heads out, and I don my suit once again and get Stalkicon prepped for patrol. I double check my weapons and ammo capacity, as well as fuel, and tires, for the proper pressure. I can't be going into battle, and possibly have a blowout, or run out of ammo.

"Ready, Night Stalker, for patrol…weapons ready…rockets ready….overall integrity one hundred percent," Stalkicon says, as I head out into the night and see what kind of trouble I can get into. There's nothing better I enjoy than to be on my super bike at 1,000 feet over the City of New York. Cold breezes are flowing through my hair, and I can hear the sounds of the city below. The city sometimes seems to take on a life of it's own from up here, if you listen close enough. Seems strange, but it's true…at least to me anyway.

"Let's head over to Manhattan, and see what is going on over there," I tell him, as he repositions himself, and heads in that direction. Manhattan is one of the areas that got hit hard by poverty and depression, and the big quake of 2012. It is rather different looking than it was ten, or even twenty years ago. Crime is heavy in this area, and so there are a lot more murders, rapes, and looting.

"Affirmative, arrival in Manhattan in five minutes," Stalkicon tells me, as I adjust my holsters and enjoy the ride over the water. The cool night breeze helps ease my mind about the incident at the prison earlier today. Something stinks with the whole thing, but I have yet to put my finger on it. If only my grandfather and father were here to help. Unfortunately, I am all alone in this venture of mine. I reestablish my mind with the current events as I see Manhattan straight ahead of me. I feel a presence in the air as we touchdown.

CHAPTER ELEVEN

The Peacemaker

Manhattan - 12:00 am

I step off Stalkicon, and as I do, I hear a bunch of yelling and noise over in one of the alleyways. The sounds of men fighting over something ...what, I am not sure yet, but I put my game face on and I draw my pistols. I then run over to check it out. I get closer, and I hear the following conversation going on.

"You put those darn TV sets down right now, you lil' scum buckets! They belong to this here store. You betta listen to me, or else," this country, twangy voice says, in the distance.

"Yeah, what if I don't want to! Then what? Watcha gonna do...country boy?"

A much younger voice, with a heavy New York accent says back, "Bring it on, pasha...you ain't nothing...let's go guys...these babies will be worth some mucho bucks to Mr. O."

"Stop right there...you little pissants...you are not taking those anywhere! Drop them right *now*," I say, as I fire a shot from my pistols into the midnight sky. "I rule these parts of the city ...you just operate here because I let you, not because I want you to."

" Whoa...its Night Stalker...I've heard about you! You know that Black Star is going to come after you, as soon as he gets out of that wretched place," the punk says to me, as he throws a large TV in my direction. "Here take it then...I'm not dumb enough to mess with the likes of you ," the punk says, as he and his buddies run off into the night.

"Hey...you okay man? I hate those little punks...but you catch them...then they just weasel their way out again...it's a vicious cycle," I say to the man in the cowboy hat. He is a big man, much taller than I am, and he has a pair of pistols on his sides.

"Name's Peacemaker...but who the heck are you...some sorta vigi...vigi," he struggles to express himself. "Some kind of superhero guy?" he says back to me as we both size each other up.

"I am Night Stalker....it seems you have your hands full over here. Maybe I can offer some assistance to ridding Manhattan of these punks once and for all," I say to him.

This guy seems to be the law over here. I mostly stay in the Brooklyn area, but I don't want to step on his toes either. The more crime we can eliminate, the better. The cops have their hands full with the everyday domestics and lost cats in the trees. We, as vigilantes take on what they think is nothing but some little punks just running around and selling drugs and stealing jewelry. They are so wrong. There is a lot that goes on in this city that they need to admit to…and deal with!

"I am doing okay…they just got the jump on me, that's all," he says, as he tries to sound like he has the situation under control. "The next time they come around here…I will be more than ready," he says, as he fires a couple of rounds into the air too. The blast lights up the alleyway, and people in the nearby buildings start bitching and moaning about all of the noise outside.

"Let's go after these punks, shall we? I need a good workout anyway," I say to him as he hesitates and waits for me to say something more. He is new at all of this, and could probably use my guidance, and my finances to better himself.

"You see, I would, but their boss, Mr. O, he's um…no pushover…if you get my drift. He makes Black Star look like a toddler! He is really big and mean, and he ain't nothing you or I want to mess with. It's best to just leave him and his gangs alone and let them…" he says to me, as I interrupt him.

"Let them rule? No way in hell am I gonna sit around and wait for some organized crime boss to take over Manhattan. It will *start* here, but it will end up being the whole world," I try to explain to him.

"That's all fine and dandy for you, but I'd like to live another day or so before Mr. O looks for me, and makes me into fish stew," he says all nervous and afraid.

"Hey…are you a superhero…or a super zero? Let's go and find this Mr. O, and show him that he can't push you, or me, around anymore!" I say to convince him that he can succeed. "Let's go back to my place, and see if we can't boost that confidence of yours huh?" I tell him as he agrees, and we go get onto Stalkicon and head back to the townhouse for the night.

CHAPTER TWELVE

Thanksgiving / Mother

November 2025

"As most of you know, tomorrow is Thanksgiving, so there will be only four hour shifts. Some of you will be on call, so keep your frickin' beepers on will ya? Go home and have a nice holiday," O'Reilly says to us, as he gets ready to finish up some paperwork.

"I guess that's it for me, oh man… Mom! I wonder what she has going on for the holiday? I guess I better head over there and find out," I say as I head out of the station and back to the townhouse. Jeff, aka the Peacemaker, should be there training with Dr. Shangli. I took him under my wing to train him better

in the arts of combat, martial arts, and firearms. He is good…
but he can get better.

Back at the townhouse, Jeff is making use of his pistols at
the firing range I installed in the basement. It can withstand
pointblank AR-15 rifle fire. I put it in so I could practice when
I felt rusty, or needed improvement. Sometimes I shoot just for
pure pleasure. I just *love* the sound of gunfire!

"How's it going Jeff? Shangli isn't being too rough on you is
he?" I say to Jeff, as he gets ready to unload both pistols on two
different moving targets. He has the willingness to learn, just
lacks the self-confidence that sometimes affects us all.

He fires off all twelve rounds into the target, with lightning
speed and determination. Only six actually are on target. The
smoke fills the air, as does the smell of gunpowder. I can see the
frustration in his eyes. He throws his pistols on the floor and starts
heading to the door.

"Hey, where are you going? So you didn't hit the target with
every shot. Not a big deal when you're just starting out. I was
like you once, before I got trained in this very same house by
my grandfather, and some by my father, before he disappeared.
It's okay," I tell him, and try to reassure him that we all make
mistakes sometimes.

"Yeah, but I'm supposed to be a crack shot, remember…I'm
the Peacemaker. How can I fight criminals and win, when I can't
even do something so simple as hit a moving target at fifty yards?
Tell me, huh! *Tell me how!*" he says, as he gets angry at himself.

He is flooded with emotions and is ready to just give up. I wish I knew about his background, but he isn't ready to open up to me yet.

"Hey, why don't we just give it a rest for today, and go to my mom's tomorrow for Thanksgiving dinner? How does that sound? She usually puts on quite a feast . My aunts and uncles will be there. I'll let her know that she is going to have three more guests. Come on, what do you say? It'll be good to get out of Brooklyn for a while," I say to Shangli and Jeff. Shangli shakes his head in agreement, and after a few minutes of silence, so does Jeff.

We all go upstairs to the guest room, and talk about our pasts for a little, before we call it a night. Of course, I can't sleep as usual. Ever since I was a kid, I have had the worst cases of insomnia. I 'm not sure exactly where it stems from, but I think it all started when my father disappeared. Funny thing about that situation, is that the police never did a very lengthy investigation. Not that I remember anyway. Then again, they had me on so many sedatives that I really didn't know if I was coming or going. All I remember is that Mom cried a lot, and told me that everything was going to be okay .

Since I have been training Jeff, and he is new to being a superhero, I just lay back and think back to the old days when my grandfather was alive. My grandmother had passed away before I was born. Some sort of rare cancer they said. So Grandpa had a lot of time on his hands. I used to go to his house every day and hang out with him. After he retired from the police force, he found hobbies to keep himself busy. On occasion though, he would have to send me home. He always said that he wasn't feeling well, or he had some place he had to be. I never questioned it, I just went back home.

Until one day when I was there, I happened to stumble upon something that would change my life forever! I was there visiting Grandpa as usual, and we were in the library room. He had so many different and rare books in there. He always told me to be careful and try not to touch too many of the books in the library, because they were very old and fragile. Kind of like me, he would always tell me, and just smile.

He was in the living room watching a football game, when I pulled out this book that had no title on the binding. When I gave it a tug, a strange noise occurred and the floor beneath me opened up, and I fell down this tube into what appeared to be the basement of the house. It was dark and creepy for a boy my age. There were all of these flashing lights and strange looking costumes, like the kind you see on Halloween. Then an alarm sounded off that made me cover my ears, it was so loud.

Grandpa came down the stairs and turned off the alarm. He looked at me, first in anger, then with a smile. He saw something in me that I never knew I had, and he knew I had potential beyond my wildest dreams.

"So....I see you went snooping...well...I guess we'll have to do something about this won't we?" he said to me, as I thought he was going to punish me for being down here in the first place.

Instead, he sat me down and started telling me a story about heroes and villains, and how our family has been fighting crime for centuries. His father before him and his father and so on, all the way back to the days of kings and queens, and knights on black horses....then I wake up, as I hear the alarm go off, and I hear Jeff and Shangli talking downstairs. It's time to get ready to go to mom's and have a wonderful Thanksgiving dinner. She hasn't seen me in months, because I have been so busy at work during the day and night. I sure hope she made that special stuffing she always makes. It's a recipe that has been handed down from generation to generation for years. I can't wait! It has the right blend of spices, breadcrumbs, and vegetables. It doesn't give you a lot of gas either. I happen to look forward to it every year.

As we head over to Mom's, we discuss where we see ourselves in the next five years. I hope to have a wife and some children . There's just one little problem though...I lead a double life. How am I supposed to explain this to a woman I love? There's no way I can ever let anyone else know my secret, except for Shangli and Jeff, who already know who I am by day...and by night.

As we pull up to Mom's, I can smell the turkey and all of the fixings that go along with it. I wish I lived closer so I could eat her homemade meals everyday. Jeff and Dr. Shangli are salivating at the mouth, as we walk up the stairs. I knock on the door . I am dressed in my police uniform, it's the best outfit I have for a special occasion such as this.

"How you doing Mom?" I say, as she opens the door and I give her a big hug. We are all standing there with smiles on our faces. Our stomachs are ready to consume this fantastic feast. Mom always has a smile on her face when she sees me walk up to her door.

"Oh my, is that you James?" she says as she reaches over to the nightstand for her glasses. " It is! My, my, how long has it been my boy?" she says as she gives me another hug and a kiss on the cheek. "I have missed you so! Who are your friends that you brought with you?" she replies, as she looks over my shoulder at my friends standing behind me.

"This is Roman Shangli, the head scientist of the New York Science Building, and this is my friend, Jeff Singer . We just met a few days ago in Manhattan. Apparently we have the same unique taste for home cooked foods, so here we are," I say to Mom as we step inside and remove our coats. It sure is a wonderful day…the weather is nice for the end of November. Not much snow on the ground either, I'm glad of that. Made getting here easier.

"Nice to meet you both. My name is Mary. I am James's mother. Please sit down if you want to. I'll get my brothers and sisters, and then we can chit chat until dinner is ready. Should be another couple of hours or so. You just can't rush my stuffing or it gets hard and dry," Mom says, as she goes down to the basement, and grabs my uncles, Ralph and George. They like to smoke and play cards when they come to visit Mom. It is quiet, and they don't have to listen to their wives talk about how they don't clean up after themselves and whatnot.

"Hey, James, are you still on the police force, or have they thrown you out yet?" Uncle Ralph says to me, as he punches me in the arm jokingly. "I heard a rumor the other day that they put you on meter maid duty! Is that true, or what?" he says, as I cover his mouth. "What …what did I do wrong?" he asks me, as I hold my hand there for a moment longer.

"Of course it's not true. He only threatened me with it. Now will you keep your mouth shut. Mom doesn't know that I got my ass chewed out by the Chief the other day. I'd rather she didn't know. Just think how heartbroken she would be. She doesn't need any more pain in her life," I say to him, as he nods his head affirmatively, and I remove my hand from his mouth.

"Sorry, kid, I didn't know. I'll do what you ask, but I can't guarantee old George there will keep that kind of secret away from your mother. He is the biggest blabbermouth there is. He should be coming up anytime now, he just had to finish his cigar," Uncle Ralph says, as he heads into the kitchen to get another drink. He is a big burly kind of fellow, with a big heart…sometimes.

"Look, everyone, it's Jimmy boy, he decided to show up for a dinner for once!" Uncle George says, as he sizes me up and puts me in his signature headlock to give me a nuggie. "Who are your friends? They look kind of sketchy to me. Let me see here," he says, as he adjusts his glasses and grabs his pipe from his shirt pocket. "We got a weird dude in a long coat here, and then we got this short little fella who looks like he belongs…" he says, as he looks at Jeff and Roman.

"Hey, be nice to my friends will ya!" I say to George, as he just shrugs his shoulders and puffs away on his pipe. Both of my uncles are retired, and served in a few wars long ago, so they can be harsh on people sometimes. Crotchety old fools , but you gotta love em for the comedy relief.

"George, hey, George, you know I don't want my house smelling with that nasty smoke when we have guests! Go put it out, and leave it downstairs!" Mom says, as she lets everyone know that dinner is ready, and everyone can come eat now.

The turkey is always carved by my Uncle Ralph. He thinks he is the king, and expert of, meat cutting or something. He was a butcher, like a hundred years ago…well …not that long ago… but long enough to where I think he invented the knife. Anyway, every year when he comes over to Mom's, he is the only one who can prepare and cut the meat. I'll tell ya, he likes eating it too!

George, on the other hand, is a little on the lazy side, but I'd never tell him that for two reasons, one, he is family, and even though he has his faults, he'd give you the shirt off his back if the needed arose. And two, it would just kill Mom if she knew all of my thoughts. That's why they stay inside of my head and nowhere else. Sometimes it is best to say *nothing*.

After seconds of the turkey that Ralph pushed in my face, and thirds of Mom's stuffing, I feel like a turkey myself. I couldn't move for what seemed like ten minutes. Mom always says I can use the extra weight, but who wants to see a fat crime fighter? Not me, that's for sure.

"Oh guys, these are my aunts, Monica and Rita," I say, as I introduce them to my friends. Monica is George's wife, she is much younger than him. She always has to pinch my cheeks when she sees me. I'm not ten years old anymore, but it pleases her, so what the heck…I guess I'm tolerant.

Rita is Ralph's wife, and she is a couple of years older than he is. A very nice lady who always slips me a few bucks here and there when I need it. She always seems to douse herself in perfume, but her warm smile always lights up the room.

"Well, you boys up for some cards or what? Old Ralph is getting too easy to beat these days and well…you don't want to listen to the women talk all night do ya…it's rather boring and makes me tired," Uncle George says to us, as he makes his way towsards the basement door.

"George, you leave those boys alone! You know that they don't come here to play cards and lose all of their money," Mom yells out, as she is doing some of the dishes from dinner. She always seems to know what's best for everybody. It is a pity she can't get George to be as enthusiastic about helping her with the dishes as he is about playing cards.

"That's okay, Mom, we have to get going anyway. We want to beat the evening traffic, and Jeff has to get home to run some errands," I tell Mom, as we grab our jackets and head to the front door.

"Well, okay I guess. You're gonna miss out on everyone talking about your dad. I know it bothers you. It does me too, but we have to talk about it and let some of that pain go. He would have loved to be here but…you know…" Mom says, as her eyes start to tear up a bit.

"I know, Mom, maybe next time, okay? We really have to get going. Thank you so much for the dinner. I'll try to make it over more often, but I have been so darn busy lately you know, with work and…" I tell her, as I make my way out the door. "I love you all, and I will see you all on Christmas Day, at my place….don't forget," I say, as I close the door.

"Yeah, whatever kid…you just didn't want to get beat again by your uncle Ralph, that's all. Remember two years ago, I was this close to owning your car, and your paycheck for a month… next time kid…be ready…I'll be taking everything but the kitchen sink…ha, ha, see ya kid…and your weird friends," Uncle Ralph says, as my other uncle and my aunts wave goodbye to us out the front window. Mom is trying to sneak in and does her best to wave goodbye to us too.

The early evening air is crisp, but soothing. Mom's house is always hot when she makes Thanksgiving dinner. Her famous stuffing, and her sweet hospitality is worth it though. I am the only person she has now that Dad is gone. She has her brothers and sisters, but it's not quite the same. Maybe I'll never know what really happened…maybe I will…when I'm ready.

I would have liked to have stayed and talked about Dad with everyone, but it just brings up old memories for Mom and I. I can take it a little better than Mom can…sometimes. She tends to breakdown and cry for days, sometimes weeks even. She really loved him. So much that after he left, she never fell in love with anyone else again.

It was just so awful when it happened. He was here one day, and gone the next. Don't get me wrong, he's not dead or anything, just....missing, I guess. No clues, no calls, no nothing! It was like he was abducted by aliens or something. Believe it or not, that's what we thought for the longest time.

I was eight when...well...I'd better not think about it all right now. I have buried that memory in the back of my mind for a while now. I think it will stay there until someday I have the time, and the strength to go searching for him. In the meantime...I have more important things to attend to.

"Hey, James, you wanna show me some more moves when we get back, or what?" Jeff says to me, as I drive down the highway towards the townhouse. Shangli is busy thinking of new weapons we could have to fight crime. If the State will fund his new project he has plans for, it will revolutionize the way we live, and will lengthen our existence here on earth.

"Sounds good, but I need to relax for a bit first. I have a busy day ahead of me tomorrow. You can either come with me, or you can stay here and develop your skills some more with Shangli. Personally, I don't think that you are ready for field work ye , but that is your choice. I'd just hate to see you get hurt.

"What...you don't think I can handle myself out there...do ya? Well, I'll show you something mister," Jeff says as he gets upset from my previous statement. "Do you think I'm just some punk kid with a couple of nice pistols huh…well…you gonna say anything?" he says, as he looks me in the eye. I guess I may have hurt his feelings, and now he thinks he isn't worth being on the same team as me or something. That is not true at all…it's just that he is still inexperienced.

"Let's calm down shall we? We'll get back to the house, have a few drinks, and discuss this in the morning. I have to report in to the station, and then make up some excuse so I can leave and do some investigation work on my own. If you know what I mean?" I say to them, as I wink my eye.

"Yeah, yeah, whatever…but you will see that I will be as good a superhero as you are…you wait and see," Jeff says, as we pull up the drive. "You shouldn't underestimate me! I can take care of myself out there. You have to trust me more. Do you trust me James?" he says, as he awaits my answer.

"Trust is a hard thing to define. I really feel that you need at least another six months of training before you are ready to head out there with me. What if I get in trouble myself ? then what? I can't save you if I need saving too! Don't you understand that?" I try to make Jeff understand as we make our way inside the townhouse.

When we get inside, we sit down in the dining room. I grab some nice glasses from the top shelf. I reach into the refrigerator, and grab the Captain Morgan, and a three liter bottle of Coke. I put my glass under the icemaker in the fridge.

"Two small cubes please," I tell it, as it drops down two perfectly shaped ice cubes that fit superbly into my glass. I do the same for Jeff.. I just love modern day technology. My fridge is the best...it can tell you when something goes bad, or if you are low on something. You can order your groceries on it, and even have internet on it too.

"Hey, Shangli, you're very quiet, do you want a drink?" I ask him, as he is deep in thought. He is always thinking of improving this, or redesigning that. I don't think the guy sleeps at night either. His mind is always on the move. He is a workaholic, and someday when he is older will have to slow it down some.

"Wha...what was that James? I'm sorry, I'm just going over some figures in my mind for our next project. It is a crime fighting boat. It will have the same capabilities as Predator and Stalkicon does. High-tech weaponry, and GPS. This one, however, will be linked to you mentally. I plan on placing a small micro chip inside of your mask, and one inside of the boat. I think we shall call it, the Demon. I will have some plans drawn up by the end of the month.

"Excellent, Shangli, but I have just one question for you," I say to him, as I sip on my drink. "Do you ever sleep at night or what...? It seems like you're always thinking about something... man you gotta relax, or you'll burn yourself out," I say to Shangli, as he grins back at me. This drink I made goes down so damn smooth, like water, I love it!

" I do relax...sometimes...it's just that. I want to see you be successful, and I want you to train Jeff here to be the best he can be," he says, as he does take the offer of pouring him a nice shot of Saki. He likes his Scotch, and sometimes he drinks Captain

Morgan with us, it depends on his mood, I guess. He is Asian after all, but one of my close and dear friends. He will always do his best to steer Jeff and I in the right direction. He is a strong believer in our cause.

CHAPTER THIRTEEN

Back to the Prison

December 2025

After a long weekend, with no pages from the station, I head back in to check with the Chief. He is, as usual, at his desk, doing whatever he does. His coffee, piping hot and standing right next to his dozen of mixed donuts from the local bakery. He is definitely a creature of habit.

"Morning, Preston. Did you have a nice weekend? I hope you're ready to work now. Do you remember our little conversation a short time ago? I'll be keeping a close eye on you," he says to me, as he puts his two fingers near his eyes, and then points them back at me. He is only joking...I hope. He does mean well...even if it is a little harsh and rough around the edges sometimes.

"Yes, sir, I was wondering if I can patrol today up near the prison. I heard that they were having some punks hanging out near there. Probably worth looking into, huh?" I say, as I go to reach for one of his donuts. Some jelly, some Boston crème, some plain!

He slaps my hand away, as he sees me out of the corner of his eye. As old as he is, he sure does have a sharp eye still...and quick reflexes. My hand is stinging as I rub it to try to make the pain go away.

"What makes you think I want to give *you* one of my *precious* donuts? You have to earn such privileges as that," he says, as he looks at me with a peculiar look on his face. "There's nothing going on up there, why are you so adamant about go? You better not be withholding any information from me boy ...or else! What do you know that we don't...huh? I sent two guys up there a couple of nights ago....nothing...but if it will get you out of my hair for a while...sure...why the hell not?" he says, as he closes up the box of donuts, and takes another sip of his coffee. "That Mrs. Bloomington ...She makes a helluva bunch of donuts...but...she needs to work on her coffee...strong...nasty...not so fresh," he replies, as I walk out the front door.

"Hey Preston, he yells, don't go trying to be a hero or nothing either. I can't send good men up there to bail you out if you get into trouble. I wish you were more like that Night fella. Now... that's a *real* cop right there. You should find out where he lives...

72

maybe take a few tips from him," the Chief says to me, as he reopens the box of donuts, and takes a bite of a jelly one. "Damn it …now see what you made me do…just get out of here…and don't break anything!"

The New York City Maximum Security Prison
9:00 am

As I make my way to the prison, I stop off and change into my suit. They won't tell any information to James Preston, the third, but they will spill their guts to…Night Stalker. I check all of my weapons, and park the cruiser on some side street nearby. I test my wrist communicator. "Stalkicon, are you ready for deployment?" I say, as I hear the underground doors open up in the background.

"Affirmative, Night Stalker! GPS tracking you now…. Prison…e.t.a. three minutes," he says back to me, as I wait for him to arrive.

The morning sun changes to clouds and snow showers, as I make my way to the doors of the prison. The gate guard is still Jimmy. He must have been here for at least ten years by now. I guess he really likes his job. Maybe that is all he has ever known… at least he is good at what he does.

"Hey, Jimmy, how's it going today?" I ask, as I see Stalkicon land in the parking lot behind me.

"G…g…good, Night, did I just see your um…motorcycle… land…na…it can't be," he says, as he can't believe his eyes. Maybe

I has been at this job too long, he thinks. So what can I do for you?" he asks me, as I watch behind me…just in case.

"Does that security guard, Rick, still work here? I would like to ask him a few questions about the Drakken murder…suicide… what have you?" I ask him, as he starts to get all nervous on me. Maybe he knows more than he should? Of course, that is just a guess."

"Um, no…Mr. Night, I mean Night Stalker, he got fired last month. I'm not sure why. He got a call from someone…came in, dropped off his stuff…and that was it. Strangest thing is that he would always change the subject when the Drakken case came up! We didn't talk about it much of course, but I never could figure that guy out. Why? Is there something wrong?" Jimmy asks me, as I rub my chin and take a deep sigh of disappointment.

"No…nothing wrong…just trying to get some more information from all the parties involved in the Drakken case," I tell him, as I walk out the door and back to the parking lot.

Another dead-end. The chief was right, there really is nothing up here but an empty prison, and old men waiting to retire. Why do they keep this place going then?

"Stalkicon…set coordinates back to the townhouse, I will meet up with you later on," I say into my wrist communicator. I think all of my work is done here…for now. I will need a really good lead in order to get back into here again.

I get back into the cruiser, and start to think about everything that just happened. For some reason, I get this funny feeling that Jimmy wasn't telling me the truth. Why would he have a reason to lie? It just doesn't make any sense. He has always been an honest older gentlemen, just working a few hours a week while he gets his Social Security. If he was lying, then he must have had a really good reason to do so. Maybe he was being provoked by another source, so he had to lie in order to stay alive. Wait a minute here …I maybe jumping to conclusions. It's just the state prison, and he is just a security officer doing his job. Maybe he was telling the truth after all.

As I head out in the cruiser off of that side street, I see a face looking out of the window in the door of the prison. He is watching me drive off. I can't make out who it is. I take out my compact binoculars, but by then it is too late. The person in the window has gone. All I see now is Jimmy waving his hand as I drive away. He doesn't look scared, or spooked or anything… just normal…maybe *too* normal, or am I jumping to conclusions again.

"You did a wonderful job, Jimmy, you get to live another day," a voice says, as he pats Jimmy on the shoulder. "I have a unique plan in store for you, my pet," the voice says, as he moves away from Jimmy. He makes a lot of noise as he moves around. A pile of hair lies on the floor near Jimmy, as the voice starts to disappear into the distance.

"You do right by me, and I will take care of you… do you hear me Jimmy?" the voice says, as Jimmy turns around and tries to reply to the voice, but it's too late.

"Yes, I will do as you ask, but it doesn't mean I have to like it," Jimmy states, as he continues to wave to Night Stalker, until he is gone from his sight. He sits back in his seat and scratches the side of his neck. There, imbedded under the skin, is a small transmitter. It itches sometimes, and is annoying as all hell. Jimmy sits back down at his desk, and stares off into space.

"Wha...wha...what just happened? Why am I at work today? Today is my day off! What is going on here?" Jimmy says, as he gets out of his chair and starts getting hysterical. He holds his head and questions the reason why he is where he is. "I gotta start laying off those pills that Marge keeps giving me," he says, as he sits back down and shakes his head. He can't remember why he is here, and even worse, and more scary...is *how* he got there. He is trying his best to figure it out, but his mind is blank.

CHAPTER FOURTEEN

84ᵀᴴ Precinct takeover

11:00 am

I take the cruiser back to the station. I suddenly get this funny feeling in my stomach as I look, and all of the cruisers are still there. No one is out on patrol! No one is out on the streets protecting the innocent. I wonder what is going on?

I bet it's the Chief, and one of his stupid, boring meetings again on protocol, and parking and blah…blah… blah. Doesn't he have something better to do with his time than rag on us for all of these little things that we're not following?

As I walk up the steps into the station and open the door, all of the officers inside are just sitting at their desks, staring into space.

They look like they are…hypnotized or something. I get out my pistol, and make my way to the Chief's office slowly, oh, ever so slowly and stealthily.

I hear voices coming from inside. The blind is closed on the door, and that is very unlike the Chief, as he likes to watch the secretaries from upstairs walk by in their short mini skirts. Sometimes he throws a pen on the floor outside his office, just so he can watch them pick it up. He is a dirty old man sometimes, but it's funny. He wouldn't know what to do anyway. His prime has been gone for a long time. He can at least drool on them I guess, and enjoy his own thoughts. Not much fun for them though.

"Hey…you can't just barge in here like you own the place… wait…what are doing? What the hell is…ahhhhhah…!" I hear the Chief scream out, as I see two shadows walking around in there.

"Now…you will do exactly as I say, and that is all…is that understood?" the voice says.

"Yes, yes, I will do your whatever you say. What is it that you ask from me…wha…who…? Oh, no, *you!*" I hear the Chief say back.

Suddenly, I hear a lot of scuffling, the Chief must be trying to fight back, and I see a gloved hand in the window. It is yellow with black stars. I hear rustling around inside and I see one of the shadows sitting down in the Chief's chair.

"Ha…ha…ha…ha… now with the police force under my command,   no one can stop *me*…ever…not even…NIGHT STALKER…..Ah, ha…ha…ha…ha…ha…!" the voice says.

I break down the Chief's door to find him sitting in his chair. The voice is gone. Everything seems to be back to normal. I hear the other officers talking outside the office just as if nothing had happened.

"What do you think you're doing, Preston, breaking down my door…that's going to come out of your pay you know…crazy kid!" the Chief says, as takes another sip of his coffee.

AUTHOR'S NOTE:

Following are a few chapters from the next book in the Night Stalker series: Black Star's Revenge, which will be out sometime in the future.

I have been busy working on it for the last year and a half, and I hope you enjoy this little prelude. Currently, as I am writing this, I have started working on ideas for the third book in the series, The Puppet Master. I hope you will enjoy this excerpt!

NIGHT STALKER II

BLACK STAR'S REVENGE

Its 2026, the world has changed, and New York City has changed...maybe I have changed. The world's economy is continuing to decline. City crime has risen 50% in the last few months. Lynching and more robberies hinder the grand city we all used to know. The police have failed in trying to stop the criminals from running good, honest, hard working people out of the city. There is a need now more than ever for superheroes to avenge the unjust. That is where I come in...

New York City - June 5, 2026

As I wake up and do my usual morning duties, such as exercising, laundry, and the chore that everyone hates the most... dishes, I turn on the TV. I see on the news program that a bank robbery is in progress. "Here we go again," I say, as I don the suit that the public recognizes so well. Being in the spotlight wasn't something I expected, or wanted to happen, it just did. I am still having some trouble adjusting to it all.

"Two armed assailants in masks, robbed the Madison Avenue Bank ten minutes ago, and got away with a substantial amount of money. They are saying over one million dollars. No one saw their faces, or was able to capture any voices on camera. They are considered dangerous and are still at large."

"O'Reilly's going to kill me...I'll be late again for sure," I say to myself as I race down the street towards the bank. Up ahead about a half a mile are the robbers. Two motorcycles are speeding along, as I start my chase after them. I push the stun missile button on Stalkicon. The missile flies after them at a high rate of speed. Right on target it lands projecting an energy that envelopes them, knocking them unconscious.

I grab the bags of cash from them as they lie on the ground bleeding and broken. I never aim to kill, only to stop the perpetrators in their tracks. Very rarely do I kill anyone with the intent to kill, if that makes any sense. Within a minute or two, the police are putting the cuffs on them and hauling them down to the station. I hand the money to the arresting officers, as I am out of time to deliver it back to the bank myself. I am already almost thirty minutes late for work.

"Thank you, Night Stalker," the officers say to me. I nod my head and smile. I start up Stalkicon again, and head off in the direction of my workplace, 84th Precinct. Five minutes later, I find a nice parking spot behind some old warehouse, out of sight, and out of mind, of the daily riff raff of this part of the city. I rush to get into my police uniform and head into the first floor of headquarters.

"*Preston!*" the voice echoes through the building, I hear O'Reilly say, as soon as my feet walk past the front door. I look at my watch, and realize that I am now almost an hour late.

"Where the *hell* have *you* been? You are on thin ice with me," O'Reilly says, as his voice rises above the typical, and often boring, office chatter. It seems that I have nearly worn out my good family name and rapport with Tom. I have been late for work for the last two months, with little or no explanation. At some point, I will have to actually try to be...*on time.*

Tim, from Interrogation, comes rushing into Tom's office as he is reaming me out, talking about responsibility, and how I can't possibly come from the same cloth as my grandfather and father before me. All of the stuff I've heard about a hundred times before. "If you're late one more time...even a second...you'll be pulling meter maid duty at the high school...you *get me* Preston?" O'Reilly says, as he looks at me very sternly, and then slams his hand against the wall. "What is it Tim, I'm busy ripping Preston a new ass?"

"We still have one of the bank robbers who robbed the Madison Avenue Bank this morning. The other one managed to escape somehow on foot! We should have him within the hour. The first one had this on him," Tim says, and pulls a metal square object out of his pocket with LED lights on it. "I'm not sure what it is, but it looks important. They guarded it until we took one of his hands and broke it in three places. After that...well,...he was ... more responsive to our questions," Tim says to O'Reilly, with a sardonic smile on his face. "Nothing like a little torment and torture for these criminals."

"I think they were stealing money to find something," I say to O'Reilly. "Maybe they have plans for something bigger in the not too distant future?"

"Shut up, Preston! You're already on my black list...you want to make it worse?" O'Reilly says, as he glares at me, his face blood red, like he was going to have a coronary.

"No! But...sir... I ... think..." I mumble and stumble at trying to find the right words to say to O' Reilly, without a sheer sense of confidence.

"You don't think, Preston, that's your problem, and why are you *so late* all the time? What is more important to you than your job, huh?" he says to me, as he is walking away in disgust.

"If you only knew, Chief," I say under my breath, as I grab the keys to my cruiser. A modernized version of a Chevrolet Impala, with hover capabilities. Its four doors are black and white, with a little more than three hundred horses under the hood.

"Good job...well done, Preston, for all the times of being late, and giving me a thousand and one excuses, you've won the prize of the month..." Here it comes, I think to myself. "Meter Maid service," O'Reilly says triumphantly, as he slaps me hard on the back. Everyone in the department laughs at me as I walk out the front door to my cruiser.

"Hey, hey, Preston, it's really a good color for you. How about a pink tutu?" Jeff Berkowitz yells, and mocks me as I make my way past him to go outside. For my humiliation, I have to wear a purple hat on my head that reads, "Meter Maid."

"Asshole!" I say under my breath, and slam the door to my police car, and prepare to drive to my new 'job' for the next … who knows…hopefully, only a few weeks.

"Officer Preston 03319, reporting for patrol…initiate meter maid duty as per Chief O' Reilly's request," I say, as the computer responds and details my destination on the screen. I adjust my seat, check my mirrors, do my routine testing of primary functions, and then drive north to the high school.

"Headquarters to 03319…come in Preston…emergency….we have a 10-75 (domestic dispute) in progress in your area, three blocks to the east from where you are now…please respond with caution!" Lisa, from Dispatch says over the speakers in my car. She then sends me the GPS navigational directions. Response time should be three to five minutes depending on traffic.

"10-4 HQ…following GPS to domestic," I say back to Lisa. I take a deep breath, and prepare for another great day in New York City…What a life!

5 minutes later – Brooklyn - Domestic Dispute

"Hey…get away from me, you cheatin' bastard! You are a *worthless* piece of crap!" a distraught female of about twenty five or so yells at her boyfriend. Or maybe ex? She is standing in the doorway of a rundown low-income, or State funded apartment building, on the outskirts of this slum area of Brooklyn.

"Let me in there, you *stupid* bitch…I wanna see my son, *now!*" the man says. He is around the same age, maybe a little younger, but still quite adamant as to what his wishes are. He is attempting to force his way into the building, no matter what the outcome is, apparently so he can see his son. I arrive just in time, as he is about to strike the woman with a closed fist.

"*Hold it right there*, sir, can you please make your way over here, we need to talk!" I say firmly to the man, as I pull up to the building. If I was a minute or two later, it would have been too late for the woman, and the situation would be different. Luckily, this is not the case…at the moment.

"*Back off*, Pig! this is between this slut, and me. You have no business here. I'm gonna see my son…or else…I'm gonna *kill* the bitch," the man says, and pulls a small knife out of his pocket. The blade glistens in the morning sun and shines in my eyes. I change my position, and refocus my attention on the couple.

"*Whoa there… freeze!*" I say to him, and pull my pistol from its holster and aim in the perpetrator's direction.

"Whatcha gonna do, copper…shoot me…? you little skinny punk…why I'll come over there and give you the beat down of your life," he says, and turns his attention to me, and then begins to walk in my direction.

Just what I wanted to start my day…some coked up loser, who likes to beat up women. I quickly prepare myself mentally and physically, then hold my pistol straight on him, aiming straight at his chest.

"*Stop!....stop this*, Rick," the woman cries hysterically, as she watches the fight that's about to unfold before her eyes.

I get into firing stance, and keep my aim steady. Rick continues to approach me, still yelling and calling me names. He looks at me, then looks back at the woman...antagonizing me to do something...to make the first move. He is walking towards me now, and waving around the switchblade in his hand. I pull back the hammer on my pistol, and get ready for the worse scenario.

"*Stop where you are*...this is your last warning, Rick! One more step and I *will* shoot you," I say to him.

He waves the knife around again, and moves toward me at a quicker pace. He looks at me, then down at his feet, and takes one more step in my direction. I see that he is unresponsive to my warnings, and trying not to put myself in danger any longer, I squeeze the trigger on my 10mm. The bullet echoes in the distance, and hits him in the shoulder with a great force. He stumbles for a moment, clutches his shoulder, and then hits the ground in agony and pain.

"You son of a bitch...you shot me, now *you're gonna die!*" Rick says, as he rolls over and gets back up on his feet, switches hands, and lunges at me with the knife. He has such rage and hate in his eyes, and with a definite intent to kill me.

I fire three more rounds, one in his other arm and two in his chest. The knife falls to the ground, and a few seconds after the echoing of the gun shots stop, I hear the woman scream at the top of her lungs in the background. As much as they hated, or thought they hated each other, the feelings were still there.

"No...nooooooo...," the woman says, and runs over to Rick's motionless and bloody body that is lying on the ground. "Why... why did you do that?" she sobbed through her tears, "he wasn't going to harm you, he wouldn't hurt a fly. He just doesn't like cops...and tell you the truth...*neither do I*!" she says, as she steps forward and takes a swing at me with a closed fist in a fit of rage and grief.

I quickly move out of the way and she loses her balance. I catch her as she collapses in an emotional heap on the ground.

"I'm very sorry, Ma'am, but I was just doing my duty! I assumed he was going to kill me first. I never intended to kill him," I say to her, as she weeps in my arms. My heart sinks to the ground as I watch her go back over to Rick's body once more, and kiss him on the forehead and hug him before I pull her away.

She gains composure for a moment and says to me, "I'm no *ma'am*, the name's Shayna, and you just shot the only man I ever truly loved," she tells me, as sadness turns to anger and disbelief again.

"Get away from me...leave me along...*just get the hell out of here*," she screams at me, while I call for an ambulance for Shayna and a coroner for Rick.

By now, a few minutes had passed, and Rick was still on the ground, spewing blood out like a volcano. He motions for me to come close to him.

"You...you...killed me, pig...all I wanted...to do was...see my son, tell him I...." he says to me. He looks up at me, grabs the lapel of my shirt, and takes his last breath.

Unbeknownst to me, during all of the commotion, I never knew his son; Jake, was watching the whole scene play out, even watching his father die by my own hand. He can see everything from the second story apartment window.

At seven years old, Jake will be forever traumatized and will build up an intense hatred against all law enforcement personnel. This will continue throughout the next few years I can only assume…if no one helps him with it now! A young mind such as his, it would be tragic if he turns to a life of crime.

As the ambulance arrives, my thoughts go again to memories of my own father before he disappeared some twenty years ago.

I was just ten years old, not much older than Jake, when dad just vanished it seemed from the face of the earth.

I had hugged him the morning he disappeared before I went to school. He hugged me back, looked down at me and smiled. He rubbed the hair on my head, as he had done since I could remember. Everything seemed fine. He was getting ready for work himself. His routine consisted of breakfast, briefcase, me, and then kissing mom, before heading out the front door to his small compact environment saver, and into traffic. I wish I would've, could've, known, that that would be the last time that I'd see him.

Dad never talked about his work, all we ever knew was that he was a scientist, who worked at a lab nearby. Everything was top secret. Everything was not to be discussed. Very similar to my own life now, secret…hush, hush…mysterious. Funny how I have followed in his footsteps…a little at least.

I still remember when dad and I would play baseball on Saturday afternoons. He'd laugh, smile, but still there was an underlying continuous stress that was wearing him down.

He would bring mom flowers occasionally, and surprise her with expensive jewelry that we shouldn't have been able to afford. The diamonds and pearls would make her smile from ear to ear.

Mom worked hard taking care of us kids. She didn't have to work outside the home, because dad brought home enough money for us to live comfortably, but we were by no means rich.

"Preston…Preston!" O'Reilly says to me, as he grabs me by my shoulder and shakes me out of my trance-like state. I must been so caught up in my own little world that I never heard the ambulance, or my fellow officers show up on the scene.

"What the *hell* is going on here? You shot the crap out of this guy! The wi…girlfriend…whatever, is coming to you like some Romeo and Juliet drama, even after you shot and killed this scumbag piece of shit…what gives? Whatcha have to say for yourself?" he yells at me angrily, like some out of control psycho.

Don't get me wrong, I respect O'Reilly very much, but his anger gets to him, *way* too often. It is not constructive.

"You cost the City money…a lot of money, where did you even fathom the thought for a moment, that you had the right to shoot this man?" he says to me, as he paces around my cruiser, and slams his hand on the hood, leaving a small dent. Something for the mechanics to fix later on!

I interrupt him, and say, "For one, he was coming at me with a switchblade like a lunatic. Two, he was attempting unlawful entry into Shayna's apartment building. Three, I am sworn to protect the innocent... and myself, against all offenders. I did what I thought was right at the moment. I did my duty! So how did I cost the City money?"

"Well, let's see hummm...you killed a man because he was attempting to cause you bodily harm, but...he didn't, so... two weeks suspension with pay for misjudgment and misuse of power...and you're gonna love this shooter with me...and that's three months of meter maid duty," O'Reilly says to me, with a condescending voice.

He then he begins to make a report on the crime scene. He then hands the paperwork over the coroners, looks at the crime scene, looks at me, and then gets back into his cruiser, shaking his head along the way.

"Oh, great Tom," I say out loud. "So what happens next time someone pulls a knife on me and lunges at me, I'm supposed to let them slice me up like a piece of meat in a food processor! Yeah, right!"

"Well, you could have disarmed him, and kept your pistol holstered! You could have done a *bunch* of things where this could have played out differently. Now his blood is on your hands. You're damn lucky that I am good friends with the Mayor, because he suggested some jail time for you, and removal of your badge, but I convinced him otherwise…now go home for today," O'Reilly says, "and get out of my sight!" He closes the door of the cruiser with a slam.

"Wonderful, see ya in two weeks ….asshole!" I say to myself, and walk over to O'Reilly's cruiser. He puts the window down and holds out his hand. I give him my badge and my gun, and walk back to my apartment about thirty blocks away!

What a great day I'm havin'…I say in my mind, as I'm walkin' down the street. I can't believe it, two weeks vacation, and meter maid service for three months. How much worse can this day get?

I make my way around a corner and into a shady part of the city, when I hear a man's voice from behind me say, "Stick em up sucker, and give me whatever you got…money…jewelry….watch… whatever you got," he says to me. I feel the cold blade from a knife being pressed into the middle of my back.

"I'VE HAD JUST ABOUT ENOUGH of people like you today," I yell at him in anger, as I twist around, and take this young punk to the ground. I lay my foot into his ribs, pick him up off his feet, and slam his sorry muggin' ass into the nearest brick wall.

"First of all, in case you don't know, I'm a New York police officer! And two, what makes you think I'd succumb my personal belongings to a skinny little worthless loser like you…now, get the outta here before I *really* get mad. You ain't getting shit from me today," I explain to him in a very stern voice. He gets up off the ground, holds his gut, and runs off into the distance up the street. I try to calm myself down, and continue back towards my apartment.

"The only thing that would top it all off is...nope, not gonna say...just keep walkin'..." I say to myself, as I get close to my block. I step inside the nearly rundown old building I live in, and step thru my door. I hit the message machine.

"No messages for you, James," the 'butler–like' voice of my machine says.

"Oh, Shit...Stalkicon is still parked in that warehouse," I say aloud. What was I thinking, I totally forgot it was still near the precinct.

"Stalkicon, can you hear me?" I say, with a sense of urgency in my voice, as I speak into my wristwatch communicator.

"Affirmative, what's your location?" Stalkicon says back to me, not knowing he could be in danger as we speak. If someone was to see him, and hear him talking, they may try to steal him or even do him harm. I speak as if he is a real person. Well, to me, he is. We've been thru a lot together, it's hard to think of him as just a machine.

"Home," I say, as Stalkicon gears up to head back to the apartment building, and into a corner of the underground garage.

"E.T.A. two minutes," Stalkicon says, as it successfully cruises down the street and changes into air mode.

Bunches of people stare for a moment into the sky, and then go about their daily business. In this day and age, no one has time to check out what is going on around them. They are all like mindless slaves, stuck in this vicious routine, never-ending; continuous; annoying and uncalled for, in my mind, but whom am I to judge?

Flying over this part of Brooklyn, Stalkicon zooms in on a particular alleyway, and picks up some homeless guy...or at least, he appears to be homeless, and selling some drugs. He is handing them to this other guy dressed in white, and donning a white fancy hat. As the lens zooms in closer, a strange symbol appears on his chest. A symbol of a tornado, or something! Stalkicon can't quite make it out completely.

"Sir, two strange men selling drugs in the vicinity of you, would you like me to distract them until your arrival, or what do you wish to do?" Stalkicon says to me, as it awaits my next command.

I put on my suit, and run up the stairs to the rooftop, just as Stalkicon arrives to pick me up.

"Afterburners, Stalkicon, to that alleyway a.s.a.p . . ." I say to him, as I hold tight to the handgrips and duck down to be more aerodynamic, and to avoid the force of the wind. The rockets fire and throw out flames about twenty feet behind me. We speed at maximum velocity until we get to our destination.

30 seconds later – alleyway - Southside Brooklyn

"Hey man! Got what you asked for...not sure what you want with these pills...they act like Ecstasy when you take them...just be careful...you didn't get them from me," the homeless lookin' guy says to the man in white.

"Well...that's for me to know, and for you to just shut the HELL up...don't be so damned nervous...no one's around...we're pretty safe here...what's your problem ....anyway? I'll take care of that for ya..." the man in white says, and pulls out a pistol from inside his jacket and fires a round into the homeless man's stomach.

"HA, HAAAAAAAAAAAA!" The man in white says, as he starts searching the homeless man for money, or whatever he can get his hands on to sell on the street.

"STOP RIGHT THERE, Scumbag!" I say to the man in white, and land Stalkicon in the alleyway. I step off my bike, and take out my stun pistols.

"Who the HELL are you supposed to be...some sort of superhero or something...ooooooh I'm scared....here, take a look at this," the man in white says, as he throws an orb of bright light at me. It lands on the ground...and then he's gone.

"What the heck? Where...did he go?" I say, with a puzzled look on my face, as I try to regain my eyesight, and my bearing all at the same time.

"Stalkicon, give me a heat signature reading, 500 yards, to 1.5 miles out from this location in a 360 degree radius!"

"Affirmative, sir,…reading…no heat signatures in this area that match the man in white's, just average citizens in their homes," Stalkicon responds back to me, and readies itself for flight mode again.

"Who the HELL was that…and where did he come from?" I say to myself, as I get back onto my bike, and do my early afternoon patrol.

"On second thoughts, let's go home to find out who this scumbag is who blinded me with that light!"

My Apartment – 4:00 p.m. – New York City

I get on the internet, and look over police records for any leads that can bring me closer to finding out who the mysterious man in white is.

"Damn it!" I say, as I get more and more frustrated by the whole situation. It's as if he just vanished without a trace, no footprint., no nothing!

"If only I had more money, If only I knew where he was, he could help….maybe…just maybe…my father," I say, as I punch his name into my computer.

"James Fredrick Preston, junior," I type in, and it gives me an address within twenty seconds or so. "James F. Preston–found–6 locations," my computer responds back to me, and shows all six locations on the screen.

One, Silicon Valley, California. Two, Arizona. Three, Utah. Four, Ohio. Five, Oregon. And the sixth is in Manhattan.!"

"Oh, that's GREAT, I gotta try to find him in six different places at the same time. How the HELL am I supposed to do that?" I say, as my anger boils up and I pick up a kitchen chair and throw it through the kitchen wall. The sound of plaster and wood can be heard throughout my whole apartment making quite a loud thud.

"HEY, what's goin' on up there?" my annoying landlord of the last few months, yells from below. She grabs a broom, and slams it into the ceiling of her rundown apartment. She doesn't like it when I make a lot of noise…or anything I do for that matter. She's got to be like a hundred by now. Sometimes I wish bad things would happen to her…but then I think of how old she is, and I put them out of my mind.

"Sorry, Mrs. Peterburger, it won't happen again," I yell back to her, as I look through the hole in my wall. Good thing the neighbors aren't home at this time, because it's my kitchen but it's their bedroom wall. OOPS!

Oh shit, there goes my deposit, I think to myself. This would be a good time for me to exit this place…take a vacation and look for my father.

I take what's left of my two weeks pay from the Chief, and head to California first. Maybe I will find the answers I'm looking for there. Maybe I will have a little peace and quiet for once. I pack up just what I need for a few days, and grab all of my bags. I put a piece of cardboard up where the hole is, and attach a note to the other side explaining that I was sorry and had a little too much to drink, and will fix it when I get home.

I open up my door, and standing there in curlers and a pink robe, is Mrs. Peterburger.

"What...what have you done to my wall? You will fix that, young man...RIGHT NOW! Where do you think you're going... get BACK here and fix this, or...or...I'll..." she says frantically to me, as I practically push her out of the way, and head down the hallway, and down the stairs to the taxi that's waiting for me.

"You'll do what? Nothing, that's what you'll do. Now, if you'll excuse me, I have a plane to catch. I'll fix it when I get back...I promise... goodbye, Mrs. Peterburger," I say to her, as I open up the front door to the building and hop into the waiting taxi.

"This is coming out of your deposit, young man...do you hear me ...do you?" she screams at me. "Ahhh...it's no use. Look at all this mess!" she says, as she shakes her head in horror, and goes back to her own apartment, sits down and watches some old episodes of 'Family Ties,'

Silicon Valley, California – 12 p.m. – June 6th

After a flight from hell (courtesy of American Airlines) I land in Silicon Valley. Here, I shall begin my search for my father. What the outcome will be is unknown to me now. I hope that N.Y.C. will be okay for a few days without Night Stalker, while I personally search for the truth to my past.

"Hey, watch it punk, get the crap outta my way!" The sound of the city taxi cab driver's outbursts, reminds me so much of home. Ah...even when you leave where you come from, something always takes you back there.

I rent a car from the local imbeciles, and head down to the nearest city hall to find an exact current address. Phone booths are extinct now, and post offices have more security and bullshit paper work to go through than the White House. That place is no use, so my only other choice is the city hall.

Ten Minutes Later – Silicon Valley – Main Street

Times sure have changed since I was a kid. Commodities we used to take for granted, we now have to fight to receive. Water has to be filtered (due to the high rate of pollution) and processed at special plants, then they are sold at a high rate to the consumers. Wages have fallen 60% under the cost of living, so buying water in a gallon jug is almost like trying to buy a new car. Carbon Dioxide in the air, and mass contaminants, have taken over the world. There are companies popping up everywhere, trying to make a buck off of, 'trying to save the world'. I know better, though. I know that most of them are hoaxes...hacks...fakes...what have you. Still people are eating this up, thinking this new 'processed' water is better for them! I know it's a lie! Like animals, people are fighting over who gets what, and for how much. It's sad that we, as a people, have lowered ourselves to this level.

I arrive at the city hall to find that it's another dead end. Information on the internet has become incredibly inaccurate and useless. Hackers are constantly breaking into sites and corrupting all the information there to increase the chaos that already exists! The public no longer care about accuracy; they care about credibility and fame. I sigh and get frustrated, but it will do no good. There is no 'real person' at the little window anymore. Everything is automated, or broken, or …just simply broken down!

As the crime rate has increased, so has a desire to destroy anything, and everything, in the paths of gangs and punks. I makes me sick when I think about it too much. What a waste of time and effort this was, to come all the way across the country… for…nothing!

"So much for California, this place is a practical joke," I say to myself, as I decide to head back home and try somewhere else. No sense of wasting anymore time here, although I'm not looking forward to dealing with Mrs. Peterburger again when I get back. Maybe Manhattan will be the place where my father has lived for all of these years, with no contact with me? I wish I knew!

"He must *know* I'm a police officer. My graduation was all over the internet," I say out loud, as I'm driving my rental car back to the airport, in preparation for my return to N.Y.C. It'll be nice, in a way, to get back to the old stomping grounds again.

"Maybe he doesn't pay attention to those things, being a scientist and all? Maybe he's rattle-headed, and just doesn't have the time," I say, as I pull up to the airport and deliver my car to the …rental company…if that's what you want to call them… losers is what I call them.

"Then again, maybe my father just doesn't care, and he hasn't for all of these years," I say, with remorse and anger in my voice.

"How was your stay here in California, Mr. Preston?" the robot attendant asks me, as I hand over the thumb-print box, and slide my card through the reader for payment. No one carries paper money anymore…actually…I don't even think the Government *makes* it anymore. Everything you do nowadays is electronic and uses fingerprints for ID. If we ever had a major blackout or something, we would be screwed up and go into immediate chaos.

"Just frickin' wonderful! Gotta love the smog and the violence, and the fact that this place is a sewerage pit, other than that… pretty good trip," I say sarcastically to the attendant, as I head to the terminal and schedule a flight back to N.Y.C.

"STOP, STOP THAT MAN! He took my diamond necklace," an old lady screams out, as I try to relax and wait for my flight. I sigh and lower my head, and then stand up.

Great, just when I thought there'd be that small window of peace, oh well, shit happens, I guess. I run into the nearest restroom, put on my suit and re-emerge into the terminal about two minutes later.

"Did you see where the thief went?" I ask, as I see someone running outside towards the parking lot. "Guess I'm getting my exercise today," I say out loud, as I'm running towards the terminal doors towards the parking area. People are screaming and running everywhere. The old lady is now hysterical and is to the point of fainting.

"Hey…that's my car, you can't do that. What are you doing to me? Ahhhhhhh, Ahhhhhh, my thumb, you cut off my…" I hear a man's voice yell out in pain, as the thief rips his thumb off his hand, steals his car, and then drives out of the parking area and is heading towards the runway.

I quickly take out my stun pistol and blast the back of the car, disrupting all electrical power, as the thief is now about fifty yards away. The car stops on the runway just as a large jumbo jet is about to takeoff. If the car had hit the plane, maybe this situation would have been worse…much worse.

An ambulance was nearby, and is attending to the man's injury, as I prepare to take the thief to the nearest police station. Just what I wanted to do with my remaining time here in California. Why can't things ever work out for me …why? Is this the price I have to pay for being the Night Stalker?

"Give your statement to the chief of police,." I tell him, after the thief is in the police cruiser. Just some punk I guess, trying to make a few bucks off the necklace. We live in such a bad place now, that you're not safe anywhere. The man is going to be okay though. The medic said they said they can reattach his thumb.

I ask the man a few questions before I head back into the terminal, hoping I'll get a flight back in a reasonable time.

"Can you tell me anything about the thief that you may have noticed? A certain tone of voice, a smell, a tattoo…anything *you* may think is not important...sometimes is VERY important," I tell him.

"Not really, ummmm...I was getting ready to get into my car after stepping out of the terminal, when he grabbed me from behind, had a knife in his hand, sawed off my thumb and got into my car. Why, you some sorta superhero in that get up, or something? Why should I trust you...just get out of here and leave me in peace, will ya," the man says, as they put him into the ambulance and are just about to shut the doors, when..."Oh, wait...ummm...he had a red bandana around the upper part of his left arm. Does that help ya at all?" the man says to me, as the EMT's wait to shut the doors.

"Yeah...actually...it does...you're the man...thanks," I say back to the man. He thanks me, and waves goodbye as the doors shut completely with a loud thud.

I return to the terminal. I see the old lady still talking to the police. She sees me and then she smiles, as I hold up the necklace and hand it to her. The police are very weary of me and keep one hand on their guns. I let them know who I am, and they seem adamant about how I look, and act at first, then they realize I'm on their side. So they back off, and go back to their investigation.

I go outside, and then to an old abandoned hangar, and change back into my casual clothes. Thankfully, no one noticed. I go back inside the terminal.

"Sir, your plane left an hour ago. We sincerely apologize for the inconvenience. Next flight is in five hours. Would you like an alternate route? How can we make your flight a more pleasurable experience?" the robotic attendant asks me with a smile on her face, as my temper flares up.

"I'm not on a plane yet...I'm stuck, HERE IN THIS SHITHOLE SURROUNDED BY MODERNIZED PIECES OF GARBAGE!" I say, as I grab the terminal attendant, and throw it over the counter and into the wall. Its head pops off, and wires are hanging down onto its torso. Sparks are flying all over the place.

"I...you....can...help...flight...canceled...ughhhhh..." the robotic attendant spits and sputters out gibberish, as it runs out of power and just lays there...motionless. Its eyes flash a few times and then...nothing!

"Thank God it's dead, what a piece of shit...what I wouldn't give for a real person behind the counter. I HATE robots!" I yell, as I look at the overpriced hunk of metal on the floor. I kick the shit out of it, and release some pent up anger on it.

"HEY, YOU...whoever you are, STOP RIGHT THERE!" I hear law enforcement officers say, as I run in the other direction. Funny...how it's the same men I talked to just a little while ago, and now they are chasing me for destroying an expensive piece of metal...go figure!

I find an old plane that's been abandoned for oh...probably twenty five years or so. I'm about three minutes ahead of the police, so I change back into my suit, and jump out of the plane, just as they are coming around the corner.

"Hey …did you see a man in a black shirt run in here?" they ask me, as I shake my head, and give them a hand in trying to find *me*.

After a little while, they give up, and decide to just write it off as "defective". I find me some different clothes, and put on a fake mustache, and then head back to the terminal booth. Maybe *now*, I can get back home.

TEN MINUTES LATER – SILICON VALLEY AIRPORT

"How long before there's a flight to N.Y.C.?" I ask another terminal attendant, with an appalling look. I'll never get used to modern technology I guess…at least not these robotic poor excuses for a real person.

"Please wait one moment, sir, checking…checking…that'll be one hour from now, sir, please wait on our comfortable benches, and enjoy our complimentary refreshments provided by the California Government," the attendant says, as I just shake my head, check my mustache, and wait for my flight.

NEW YORK CITY – 2:00 P.M. JUNE 7TH

After a layover in Texas of ten hours, I finally arrive back home. I wearily carry my luggage up the stairs, and into my apartment. There are two men working on the wall I destroyed before I left. They place the sheet rock where it belongs, and are startled by my barging into my own place. They look at me for a moment with a blank look on their faces, and then get back to work. I faintly hear some footsteps coming down the hall. I hope it's not who I think it is. Then the door to my apartment flies open.

"Where have you been? You have cost me a ton of money… labor…materials! Well, what you got to say for yourself, huh…?" old Mrs. Peterburger says to me, as she is waiting for me to speak.

I look at her with disgust and say," Hey…I just got back from California, and you have to come down here and ride my ass about some old beaten up, crappy piece of wall, in your rundown stinking apartment building! I ain't got the patience, or the time for you, so just fix it …send me the bill…and then we can discuss what I WILL DO about it …you got it?" I yell at her, as I get out my work clothes, and get ready to head down to the station. Peterburger leaves, and flips me the bird.

"Old Bitch!" I say, as the workers just laugh, and go about their business.

"How much longer before it's done guys? I'd like some peace and quiet," I say to the men through my open bedroom door, as I adjust my badge and walk out the door.

"Two or three hours at the most, we can get it done today!" the workers tell me, as I close the door behind me with a slam.

84th PRECINCT – 2:30P.M.

"Attention all officers! Large explosion on 15th street, near the docks and metal factory. Ten masked men in black, and one in white. Proceed with caution. Not much is known other than they took something from inside the factory, and took off towards Manhattan," the dispatch says over the speakers inside the precinct.

"You heard her boys and girls! Let's get out there and find these punks before they get too far!" O'Reilly says, as he grabs a double-barreled pump shotgun from the wall. It's too bad he still thinks old school weaponry. It's just his style I guess.

"Dispatch, do we have any officers in the vicinity of this factory?" O'Reilly says, as he heads towards the front door.

" No one! Well...Preston is in the area...but isn't he still on suspension?" Dispatch says back to the Chief.

"DAMN IT, Preston. Even when you're gone...I'm still pissed off at you," the Chief yells.

"How much longer till he comes back on the force? Oh yeah, he'll be doing meter maid duty anyway." O'Reilly thinks for a moment, and then he says, "Maybe I was too ha...nah...he's gotta learn a lesson the hard way...my way," the Chief says, as he heads to the cruiser.

"Call him, we can use him this once...then he's back on suspension," he says back to Dispatch.

"I'm on it, Chief!" Dispatch says back, and then tries to get me on my cell, and my home phone.

I'm on my bike, so I can't reach for my...oh shit...my cell. I realize that I must have left my cell phone on the plane, or maybe back in the California airport...hopefully it is here in New York. I re-route myself, and head to the New York Airport terminal.

"Grab that metal thing over there, you maggots, or I'm taking ten percent out of your pay! Move it, do it *now*, get to the boats before the pigs come," the man in white says to his goons, as they all take a hold of this large metal frame and bring it to the boats at the docks. It appears to be able to hold something heavy and of extreme value.

"If you shitheads don't do what I say, I will rip out your throats and shit down your necks...now, let's move...quickly...quickly now," the man in white says with a harsh voice.

They break down the frame, and load it in pieces onto the boats. They load the last piece on and they hear the sounds of sirens in the background. They pay no attention and start the engines. They take off leaving a large wake behind them, and are about 500 yards away from the docks. The chief and about twenty officers surround the stairwell, and upper wall. The Chief sees the boats in the distance and fires four rounds at them. The rest of his men follow suit, and empty their pistols. The boats are too far out, and out of range, and within seconds are gone completely out of sight. The Chief is pissed and punches one of his men in the face, knocking him hard to the ground.

"Damn it...what the heck...get me the Coast Guard...and get me a drink already...I can't believe they got away," the Chief says, as he helps Stan back to his feet.

"Sorry there, Stan...I'm a little upset right now...what the HELL did they take anyway...let's check this out!" the Chief says to his men, as they approach the factory with extreme caution. The Chief looks at his watch, shakes his head, and waits for his scouts to assess the area.